GUILTY PRIDE

Lisa Quinn

authorHOUSE®

AuthorHouse™
1663 Liberty Drive
Bloomington, IN 47403
www.authorhouse.com
Phone: 1 (800) 839-8640

Published by AuthorHouse 01/07/2019

ISBN: 978-1-5462-7020-1 (sc)
ISBN: 978-1-5462-7019-5 (e)

Library of Congress Control Number: 2018915032

Print information available on the last page.

This book is printed on acid-free paper.

PROLOGUE

Shorty

I tiptoed down the hallway, trying not to make a sound. I wore only my lace underwear and a tank top. A part of me felt satisfied. A part of me felt ashamed. I knew what I had done. Of course, I knew it was foul. I knew sleeping with his best friend was beyond betrayal. I knew doing this in our house, while he was there, was past disrespectful. The liquor, late hours, and slick remarks played into my decision to fuck his business partner.

I crept to our bedroom door like a thief in the night, hoping he hadn't awoken yet. He was pretty tired and drunk from the party we threw earlier in the evening. It was a celebration in honor of a successful first year for the company he and said business partner just recently established. I took a deep breath as so many thoughts crossed my mind. I turned the doorknob and quietly entered the bedroom. It was the first time I had been with another man. C was my first. He and I had been together for six years. C was all I knew. I met him at seventeen, and he was nineteen. He was my first love, my first kiss, my first everything. Yes, C made me happy. Yes, C satisfied me. Yes, C was successful. C was beginning to travel more and plant the seeds for his business to flourish. I had recently started to feel like I was missing out on something. I felt the need to explore. I wanted more. I had been with C from teenager to womanhood. I was still learning about myself and the world. I never imagined my thoughts and feelings would land me in the arms of his friend. But Duke would always say something subliminal and lately I'd been receptive.

I quietly crept across our bedroom to my side of the bed. C was still asleep. He was stretched out over the covers in only his black Versace boxer briefs. I could feel regret. I felt guilt. He began to shift positions in bed. I tried to slip in quickly. He reached out for me, and I could only go to him. I snuggled up under him in my little nook. I then began to panic. I was so in a hurry to rush back to bed I didn't think to wash up. *Please don't let him wake up*, I prayed as my head hit the pillow.

He kissed my shoulder as I laid under him. He embraced me tightly as he held me in his arms. He then began to sniff me.

Oh my God, I thought in panic. Fear and anxiety ran through my body. I could feel that he knew something wasn't right.

He immediately sat up in confusion. I could feel him looking at me. I tried not to look up to him as I continued to lie there. I could feel what he was thinking. I knew what was coming. Before he could form the words to ask or say anything, we both could hear tires screeching from the front yard. I then looked up to him. He looked at me, puzzled.

Before I knew it, he jumped out of the bed and ran to the balcony. He opened the balcony doors and watched the familiar car speed out of our long driveway. I knew then I had made the biggest mistake in my life. I quickly ran to him to try to explain. He went to the drawer to retrieve a pair of sweatpants and a T-shirt.

I attempted my plea as he put on his pants. "Baby, let me explain ..." I tried to get the words out as I approached him.

He pushed me to the floor as he stormed past me. I hit the carpet hard. I could feel the tears building in my eyes as a huge lump formed in my throat. I went out to the balcony and saw him jump in his car and speed out of the driveway.

I knew I had to stop him. I rushed for my slippers and a robe and then ran through the hallway and down the stairs. I grabbed my keys and jumped in my car. Luckily, our three-year-old daughter, Cori, was with her aunt Vicki for the night. I could barely see straight as tears flooded my face. I grabbed my car phone and attempted to call C as I went on a high-speed chase to try to stop him.

What was I thinking? Why did I do this? Why did I believe Duke? I asked myself as I accelerated down the highway. I never thought about the consequences. I never considered how this could play out if he found out. I guess that's the thing about cheating. You never consider the then, only the now. It was selfish of me to jeopardize my relationship, my family, for a quick fuck. I never considered losing anything in gaining a night of nothing.

I could feel the humiliation as I tried to keep up with C. He was too fast. I could see from his reckless driving he was on a mission to get Duke. I continued to call—no answer. Of course, he's not answering. What would I say if he did answer? "I'm sorry, C," would never be enough.

I couldn't keep up with him. I could only pray he couldn't keep up with Duke. I tried to finesse through the late-night traffic, although with tear-filled eyes, nervous hands, and a heavy heart, it was impossible. When I looked up, I realized how close I was behind an eighteen-wheeler. Before I could brake properly, the massive freight truck did.

PROLOGUE

C

Damn. Here I was doing ninety miles an hour, chasing a nigga I once called a brother. I could only shake my head in disbelief. I clutched the wheel tighter and maneuvered through traffic. I was trying my best to get closer.

"How could she? In my house?! While I was there?!" I yelled as my foot pressed harder on the pedal. "I've loved this girl for six years now! Faithful and loyal to only her! Then she fucks my nigga ... my partner ... my friend." I screamed the words as I blazed down the street. "We got a fucking family!"

My thoughts continued to race, as did I. I could picture Duke fucking Shorty. Kissing her. Touching! *My* Shorty! I thought I saw Shorty in my rearview, but that was miles ago. My only goal was to kill this nigga. This was past disrespect. A man I considered a friend would do this pretentious shit? My college buddy would do something so indecent? Celebrating our company, and you fuck my woman? In my house once I'm sleep?! I scoffed at the audacity.

I continued to ignore the calls from Shorty. There was nothing she could say to me right now. As I tried to gather my thoughts, I realized I was close enough to ram him, so I did. His car spun out of control as I hit my brakes. I could see fear in his eyes as his car spun on the pavement and ran into the median. Luckily, being almost four o'clock in the morning, the streets were empty.

The car phone finally stopped ringing. I parked, got my .380 out of the glove compartment, and exited my car. I looked around to peep the scene as I approached his car. I could hear sirens. Immediately, I ducked and tried to hide my pistol, thinking they were headed here. *That fast?* I thought. But they continued to drive past. As I moved to his car, I could see he was pretty banged up from the impact. I didn't give a fuck, though. I was boiling with frustration and anger. I wanted to implement my emotions through my fists and express them to his face. So, I punched a half-conscious man.

The sirens increased as more ambulances, fire trucks, and police flew by. I swung his door open and pulled him from the car. I threw him onto the hard concrete. At that point, I had no past—no connections to this nigga. He was now an enemy. My only objective was to hurt him as much as I was hurting. I wanted to kill him. I kicked him in the guts as thoughts crossed my mind. I punched him until I couldn't feel my fists anymore. The pain he felt still didn't surpass the pain and betrayal I felt. He lay stiff and bloody on the pavement. I jerked him up by his collar as I punched him in the mouth. His head practically dangled as blood gushed from his lip and mouth. I held him by the collar as I pulled the gun out and held it to his temple. My knuckles bled as I gripped the pistol tighter. I wanted to end his life. I wanted to murder him due to level of disrespect he had just caused.

But then I remembered—I had a daughter. I had a family and a future. I slapped the pistol across his head, and he fell to the ground. I walked back to my car and opened the door, and the phone began to ring uncontrollably again. I knew it was Shorty calling, begging for forgiveness.

I looked at my bloody, swollen hands and then looked over as Duke lay unconscious and brutally beaten on the side of interstate. I was ready to tell her what she had done. I was ready to inform her what her actions had caused. *Cause and effect … That's law!* Painfully, I reached for the phone.

"Hello? C, you there?" I could hear Tony speak into the receiver. It was her father.

It was odd that he was calling me. Shorty must've went to her dad's. *I hope she gave him the whole story while she over there venting*, I thought.

"C! Shorty has been in an accident! Is she with you!? What's going on?" he cried.

After hearing those words, I dropped the phone.

CHAPTER 1
Three Years Later

"Nice tent," I said, nodding my head toward his tall, erect manhood.

"Huh? … Oh shit," he responded, trying to pat it down.

It was C's weekend to get Cori—Cupcake to us. They had fallen asleep on my living room floor playing while I was cleaning. I had caught myself daydreaming as I watched him sleep. C was always so fine to me. His chestnut-brown complexion reminded me of a roasted almond. Below dark eyes and thick eyebrows, his low-cut beard enhanced his sexiness.

Here I go again, admiring what I can't have anymore, I had thought. Our great friendship was the only thing that had outlasted our breakup. "You can get on the sofa if you like," I offered.

"No need. I was just about to get up anyway," he told me, rising to his feet. "Where's Cupcake?" he asked, glancing around the room for her.

"Still asleep. I put her in my bed," I answered.

We both took a seat. There was space between us on the sofa. It was awkward sitting in a room alone with him. It was usually us and our daughter—or us and anyone, for that matter. Before my mind could start racing, I asked, "What you got planned for today?"

"Not much. Maybe get a bite to eat, go to the park."

I looked nowhere in particular, as I could feel him staring at me. I could feel his glare on the side of my face, like heat from the sun. I didn't have on any makeup, but he still looked at me as if I were as beautiful as the day he had met me. I now hated for people to stare at me. It reminded me of my scars. Of course, those scars reminded me of that tragic night. I wore four three-inch scars on my face: one above my left brow, one under each eye, and one on the right side of my chin. That night had left me with an ample amount of baggage to carry on as the modern-day bag lady. Along with the infamous Coach, Chanel, and Fendi handbags, that night had left me with scars, regrets, broken bones, and crushed dreams. That act of temporary pleasure had created permanent misery.

"So how is everyone?" I asked, curious to know.

"Everyone is good," he told me. "They still ask about you. When you going to visit?"

Never, I wanted to answer but kept to myself. It seemed every time I went around his colleagues and staff, I would get *the look*. Most wouldn't even attempt to look at me. It was always just awkward. During our three years apart, I began to hate myself for that stupid mistake. I had fucked over the perfect man, the perfect life, and the perfect future for a mediocre fuck. I would find myself deep in tears on many a night—hell, sometimes mornings. I suffered with severe depression and anxiety because of my selfish decision.

It's fucked up to live with the fact that *you* screwed up your happiness. But what can you do? You can't take back the past. You can't take back your choices. All you can do is live with them. I lived with the pain each day that my life could've been different had I not done something so foul.

"I'm not sure. Soon. Maybe," I lied. If I didn't have a reason, I wouldn't leave my house, and stopping by his office was not a reason.

"Cool," he mumbled lowly. I felt so tense around C. Again, awkward silence. "I see you still hitting the gym," he complimented.

"Huh," I said, being interrupted from my thoughts.

"I said, I see you still hitting the gym," he repeated.

"I don't. I run when I take Cupcake to the park. But that's it," I reported happily. I then began to blush. It felt good that he recognized my body. C always adored my shape. He had once been infatuated with my curves.

"Oh shit, you blushing," C joked, leaning toward me.

"Maybe," I stated, showing a small smile. My smile was my greatest asset. Beyond the wounds, I still had my beautiful smile. I was blessed with beauty. And genes, a decent diet, and regular exercise had my body right. Though I would never subject myself to my outer beauty, my inner beauty shined through my beautiful, one-dimpled smile. Cupcake's yell for her mommy brought our brief moment to a halt.

"I'll get her," C stated following her cry.

I then picked up the remote to channel surf, and my phone rang. "Hello," I said.

"What's up, girl?" I heard over the receiver. I then recognized the squeaky voice as my homegirl Jaz, short for Jazmine. We had met in junior high school. Jaz was a firecracker—a loose cannon. She was violent and argumentative by instinct, but you wouldn't suspect such behavior if you saw her. She was fair-skinned with dark, wavy hair. Her five-foot-six, petite frame only complimented her cute baby face. Jaz was cool and crazy. She was very private about most aspects of her life. After we graduated high school, she had just disappeared for a few years—no contact, no explanation, nothing.

"Did this wench just hang up on me?" she squeaked on the other end.

"No, I'm here, girl," I mumbled back. I could hear her coughing, so I was sure she was smoking.

"So, what you getting into tonight, Shorty? It's been a while since we stepped out. Let's go floss at the club! I got Henn! I got smoke," she gladly offered.

"No thanks, girl. I'm cool."

"Don't act as if yo' boring ass got something to do. Come on, Shorty. Live a little," she begged.

I didn't want to go out with Jaz. She was my friend for sure, but every time we stepped out, there was commotion. Unlike my other homegirl Shay, Jaz went out looking for trouble. Shay was a little older and laid back. She was about her money and enjoyed the nightlife as well.

"You should come on out! Shay coming, and she got everything planned," Jaz continued.

Damn, I thought as I held the phone. I remembered Cupcake was in my bed napping, and C had gone to get her. I forgot I had slept in his old T-shirt the night before. It was lying on the edge of my bed. I knew it was too late to stop him or hide it. *Damn,* I thought again. *I know he thinks I'm miserable now.*

"I should come over there and beat yo' ass," Jaz threatened.

I laughed a little to brush off her statement. "You need to stop. I believe you."

"Well, okay then."

As I placed the receiver on the base, C came from the back with our daughter. I was looking away, hoping he wouldn't bring up anything he had seen in my bedroom.

"Well, we 'bout to bounce," he announced, holding our six-year-old daughter in his arms.

Her long legs dangled as he held her. I enjoyed seeing them together. The love he had for her, and she for him, was priceless. With all the mistakes I'd made in life, I knew she was the one thing I had done right. My heart smiled.

"Did you want to roll?" C asked.

"Oh no," I answered him.

"Why not, Momma?" Cupcake asked just as innocently as her stare.

"Because ..." I paused. "I'm having company," I lied. Glancing at C, I sensed a bit of jealousy, or maybe I just wanted to. It used to turn me on to make C jealous. For some reason, I loved for him to express his jealous side. His anger and voice would make me want him so badly. Arguments would end up in awesome sex. And in some crazy way, I felt how much he loved me. In a wink, I missed that. I missed C.

"Okay, Momma. Bye. I love you," Cupcake told me, waving and blowing kisses.

"See you later, baby. I love you too." I walked over to smother her in kisses. "Have fun and be sweet, my Cupcake," I yelled on their way out the door.

Shortly after they left, the feeling of loneliness began to creep up on me. I experienced this sensation most of the time, and to rid it, I would endlessly clean. Only problem was my house was spotless. Before I could release any tears, the telephone rang.

"Hello."

"You heffa," a familiar voice spoke into the phone.

"Oh, so now I have to hear it from your mouth too," I said, getting comfortable on the couch.

It was my dear friend Christian TaShay, also known as Shay. She was mostly known for only dating fellas with commas in their bank accounts. Her attire mainly consisted of designer threads that revealed way too much in order to attract her next trick. Shay was intriguing. She had smooth skin the color of gingerbread. She had a voluptuous body and stunning face to match.

"You damn right you got to hear my mouth! I got our night all mapped out! VIP passes, you a bomb outfit, and even transportation," she fussed. "Now go a take a bath, shower, hoe bath, whatever—we are on our way! If we got to come kidnap you, I bet you going to the club!" She then hung up the phone.

Here we go again, I thought, looking at the receiver. I pondered if I should go with them as I hung it up. I really wasn't feeling the motivation to go to a club tonight. I had a feeling in my gut I shouldn't, but maybe tonight wouldn't be so bad.

After getting out of the shower I examined my naked body in the mirror. My curly brown hair was soaking wet. My light brown eyes burned in my reflection. My 36C breasts sat up. My waistline was still small and slim. My abs looked good, and my legs were toned. My body was still banging. My caramel skin glistened in the bathroom lighting.

Maybe this won't be so bad after all, I thought. Stepping forward and opening the door, C stood before me in the doorway. I was shocked, surprised. I was completely naked and wet, and C stood before me. I felt vulnerable, so I covered as much of my body as I could with my arms.

"No, baby, I want to see all of you," he told me, pulling my arms from my body.

I was surprised to see that he'd come back for me. I then felt overwhelmed with emotions. Emotions and feelings, I thought were long gone.

"You are so beautiful, and I love you, Shorty. Come here," he told me with open arms.

It felt unreal. I was happy. Stepping forward to meet his arms, there was a knock. I walked over to meet his open arms. With each stop I took, there was a knock. I opened my eyes and realized I'd fallen asleep on the couch. I sat up to focus, and the knocks became louder.

"Open the door, Shorty! We know you in there," they yelled from outside.

I wish I stayed in a gated community like C has been insisting forever, I thought as I got up to open the door. Shay and Jaz stood there on my front porch.

"Come on. We don't have all night," Shay ordered, pushing past me.

They were both dressed and pressed for the night. As usual, Shay was dressed to kill. The way she rocked those jeans, to the common man, were a crime. The cowboy hat and boots only accentuated her sexy cut flannel top to complete her sexy Southern girl look. I also noticed her new hairstyle of waist-length braids, which she'd gotten on her recent trip to the islands.

"You like?" she asked, spinning around. "I'm straight-up cowgirl tonight!"

"I'm digging it," I admitted.

"She should be on a horse," Jaz joked, walking to the back.

Jaz's sultry olive-green dress made her petite body look curvaceous. Her up-do hairstyle brought fun to the outfit, and the gold stilettos made the dress more seductive.

"Whatever. This style is mine, and I look good," Shay told her with a playful eyeroll.

I laughed at them both, locking my door and then following them to my bedroom. "I haven't taken a bath yet," I announced, entering my bedroom.

They both glared at me. "Well hurry up and take a quick shower. We don't have all night," Shay declared, setting shopping bags on the bed.

"You should have been bathing instead of finger fucking yourself, Shorty," Jaz teased, sitting on the chase.

"Not this time," I replied. I took a rapid shower and hurried out of the bathroom. I then sat at my vanity table as I put my hair in a ponytail. I didn't wear my hair off my face much. In a way, I hid behind my big hair. Well, at least I thought I hid the scars. Looking at my bare reflection in the mirror, I took a deep breath and prepared myself for my makeover.

Shay applied flawless makeup, and Jaz flat ironed my hair into a sexy style. The Gucci denim skirt hugged my ass just right, and the Dolce & Gabbana lace spaghetti-strap top obeyed even more. The sexy Manolo Blahnik stilettos finished my sexiness and increased my height by at least six inches. Eventually, we were ready.

Walking toward the front door, I asked, "Which club we going to?"

"Well, first we headed to my house because the limo Will ordered for us is there," she stated, rushing out the door. "Then we'll go to Silhouette to meet them."

"Them?! What do you mean *them*?" I asked, stopping in my steps.

I hated when she did that—grouped us with her friend's friends. It was like she had the best candidate, and we had acquaintances of the runners-up—not even the runners-up. Shay rarely brought dates for Jaz. Jaz's date would always end in an argument. But of course, she had some goofy guy for me.

"Calm down, Shorty. It's this real nice, very handsome gentleman. I think y'all may hit it off," she said convincingly. "He's not even from here. He's new to the city. He's different, way better than the last scrub. My bad on that."

"You say that every time, yet he be tore up from the floor up."

A small laugh escaped Jaz. "Come on, Shorty. Watch. He may be the one to change your life. And if you not feeling him, I'll be sure to dismiss him immediately," she promised.

"Okay," I agreed as we hopped in her red Mustang.

I found myself glancing in the mirror. I've rarely found time to admire my beauty—at least what was left of it. My hair blew in the wind as I thought to myself, *Makeup does wonders.* You couldn't identify a scar on my face if you looked hard enough. I could feel my excitement and confidence rising on the way to our first stop. I felt a mood coming over me, which could've been the potent marijuana Jaz lit up. I felt lovely by the time we reached Shay's condo. I smiled to myself as I exited the car, knowing I could feel sexy again. *Maybe I could do this more often,* I thought. *Maybe.*

We only waited a few minutes before a black stretch SUV pulled up. "Come on, y'all," Shay demanded, signaling for us to get in.

The driver opened the door, and we entered the luxury vehicle, which was filled with roses and Cristal. Shay's newest lover had it decked out for us, and we took full advantage of his generosity. We finished Jaz's joint and almost a whole bottle of champagne by the time we pulled up at the Silhouette.

I stared at the magnificent building like I'd never seen it before. The club was huge and was the hottest spot in the city every weekend. We peeped the scene once we exited the huge vehicle. It was packed.

We never waited in line, being with Shay. We were VIP everywhere we went with her. I enjoyed those perks when I did decide to step out. The jealous glances were normal as we walked to the front of the very long line. My confidence continued to cultivate. There was barely enough elbow room as we made our way to VIP. We had to calm Jaz down nearly three times to keep her from starting shit. Finally, we reached VIP. The atmosphere was mellow and not crowed at all. Luxury couches, lavish chandeliers, fish tanks, and reserved tables made the room look sophisticated. The crowd was chic and not rowdy. The bar was beautiful and dignified. We reached our reserved table, and immediately, our server came. She arrived with glasses of champagne with strawberries on the side.

As we sat, looking pretty, Shay thanked the young lady. We toasted and took our first sip. The server politely nodded and left us to enjoy our night.

I felt good. I looked good. *Tonight, will be great,* I thought as I sipped my glass of bubbly. "So where is this Will?" I quizzed Shay, noticing three handsome gentlemen entering the room.

"Don't speak too soon," Shay answered, also taking notice of the guys.

They were now walking in our direction. *That must be them,* I thought. For once, they all looked decent.

Jaz was finishing her glass and prepared for another when the attractive trio approached our table. The fellow on the right end was so fine, I'd end my celibacy right then and there if he were mine.

"Hey, baby," Shay greeted, standing to her hug her man in the middle.

What?! The finest one isn't hers? I thought. *Hope he for me.*

"Ladies, this is Marcus, Will, and Ryan," Shay introduced, then vice versa.

Don't get me wrong. Will and Marcus were attractive, but Ryan was downright fucking sexy. He was light skinned with light eyes and a sexy crown. Revealing a brief smile with deep dimples, I also acknowledged a boyish charm. He had curly hair and kissable lips. Under the designer button-up and black slacks, I could picture a well-toned body. My thoughts began to become a bit erotic. It had been a very long time since someone I'd just met had made me feel this way.

"Ryan, this my girl Shorty. Why don't you guys mingle," Shay stated, winking at me.

I felt excited and nervous at the same time. He sat down next to me, and the pure aroma of him made me want to melt in his arms.

"Hey, I'm Shorty," I greeted with my hand extended.

He lightly shook and softly kissed the back of it as he stated, "Hello, Shorty. I'm Ryan Vaughn. Wow. Your beauty is breathtaking, and your hands are so soft." He rubbed my hand before letting go.

"Thank you."

Just my luck. He had fresh breath and all white teeth—intact. That was a major turn on for me. Nowadays, most guys didn't care about oral hygiene unless it meant filling their mouths with gold, platinum, and diamonds. I appreciated a man with all beautiful white teeth. I admired his charm and good looks.

"So, they call you Shorty. What's your real name?" he asked.

"Sydney."

"Sydney … I like that. I'll just call you Sydney."

"Oh, so you're just confident it's going to go past this night, huh?" I replied, sipping from my glass.

With a grin, he responded, "Well, I meant for the night, but I would love seeing you again."

With my foot in my mouth, I commented, "We haven't talked for five minutes, and you're certain you want to see me again?"

"Well, I did say *see* you again. You're so gorgeous. I could just stare at your beautiful face over a nice dinner anytime," he declared, taking a quick look at my cleavage.

I lightly laughed at his swift gesture and cute compliment. The conversation rolled on smoothly after that. We talked about everything. He told me about his job in IT and upcoming ideas and projects. He explained how technology was going to change everything. He informed me he was new to the city and had just recently relocated here. I was surprised to learn that he was single and moved here alone. Well, at least that's what he was telling me. We connected on a level, and I welcomed the new feeling he was giving me.

Will had the Cristal flowing like water, and we snacked on endless hors d'oeuvres. It even appeared that Jaz was enjoying her encounter with Marcus. I could feel the buzz. After stuffing my mouth with a jumbo shrimp, I insisted everyone hit the dance floor. I felt seductive as I led Ryan to the dance floor with me. The speakers pumped a contagious tempo, vibrant voice, and Jamaican beat. I was ready to seduce him through dancing. We hit the floor and danced like long-lost lovers. I winded my hips against him, and he grinded back.

He kept in rhythm with me, and his eyes were locked with mine. "I like the way you move," he whispered in my ear.

His face felt good against mine. His rugged facial hair was a turn on as it rubbed against my cheek. "Likewise," I replied, wrapping my arms around his neck.

His feet made all the right steps, and his hands did nothing out of order. No one else mattered as I danced with Ryan. We bumped bodies to a few more tracks before we made our way back to the VIP section.

I am truly enjoying myself, I thought as we returned to our table. I requested water as I took my seat next to Ryan.

"You ladies enjoying your evening?" Will asked the table as he poured more champagne for everyone.

"Yes, baby, everything is lovely," Shay gushed as she kissed him on the cheek.

The server returned with my water. Before I could take a sip, Shay did her usual and ordered a meeting in the ladies' room. Of course, this was routine. She could tell us about her trick and question us about our potential ones.

Ryan softly touched my hand before I left the table and smiled at me. I shyly smiled back and enjoyed the feeling he was giving me. I think I felt butterflies.

We excused ourselves and left for the ladies' room. The place seemed even more packed, and the crowd was crunk. There was a totally different atmosphere in the main area.

On our way to the ladies' room, two females mistakenly bumped into Jaz! "Watch where you going," they told Jaz, continuing to walk.

"No, you watch where the fuck you going," Jaz threatened.

The females brushed Jaz off as if she was playing, but Shay and I knew the truth. "Calm down, Jaz. Fuck them hoes," Shay insisted, giving them a nasty look.

"You see a hoe, beat a hoe," the overweight one stated, standing like she was invincible or something.

"You think I won't?" Jaz said, walking toward the girl.

I wasn't ready for this drama—not yet. I wasn't finished mingling with Ryan. I grabbed Jaz before she reached the girl.

"Shorty, let me go! This bitch trying to test me," she shouted, trying to get free of my grip.

Over the loud music, I tried to convince her to calm down. That was not working. She was heated, ready to explode and beat somebody's ass—even if it was mines!

"Jaz, please don't dwell on them hoes. We'll take care of them later. 5-0 over there," I told her, nodding in the direction of security.

"So, fuck the police," she hollered, sounding like the missing female member from N.W.A.

They seemed to glance but didn't come over. I couldn't afford to miss out on getting to know Ryan. It had been so long since I'd found myself interested or attracted to anyone. The night was going so well for Ryan and me. There was something about him—something I didn't know but wanted to find out. I wasn't ready for the night to end.

Jaz still appeared angry, so I whispered in her ear, "I know we will see them before we roll out. We'll get those hoes later. I promise."

Luckily, that worked. She nodded and continued her stroll to the ladies' room. *I hope that promise doesn't come back to haunt me*, I thought, as we entered.

"So, it looks like you're enjoying your time with Ryan," Shay said, touching up her lip gloss. Will had kissed it all off.

"Yeah, he decent," I admitted. Shay really kept her word this time. He was different.

"See, I told you! He fine, a gentleman, and the fact that he got a six-figure income doesn't hurt either," she stated with a wink. "Shit," she suddenly yelled, looking at her cell phone. "What the hell he want?" She then turned to me. "Let me use your cell."

After searching through my purse, I found it and handed it to her. She dialed the digits, put the phone to her ear, and greeted the person. "Hey, boo … I missed you too … No … I'm at, uh. … All Night … Yeah, okay. I'll see you then … Love you too." She hung up, rolled her eyes, and mumbled, "He's so annoying."

"Wait, didn't you just lie like you're at All Night?" I questioned her.

"Uh, but of course. Why would I tell him which club I'm really at?"

I could only shake my head. How did she do it? Have all those guys, wealthy guys at that, doing whatever she wanted. I knew I didn't have the courage or the game to try to play multiple guys at once. I would find it hard trying to harbor feelings for someone and consistently lie to everyone. I've only been in one monogamous relationship in my life, and I horribly ended that trying to cheat.

"You cool, Jaz?" I asked, noticing her silence. I could feel her energy, and I could tell she was aggravated.

"When we taking care of that?" she asked without even looking at me.

"Let's go back to the table," Shay announced, holding the door open for us.

I grabbed Jaz's hand, and we exited the bathroom. I knew I would have to hold her hand to keep her from running off looking for trouble. We weaved through the thick crowd. *Damn*, I thought and stopped in my tracks. My feet couldn't move. They felt cemented to the floor. Right before me were Shay and Duke. Shay was standing in front of me talking to Duke! She pointed in my direction with a smile and continued her stroll to VIP.

I couldn't believe I was looking at Duke. It had been three years since I last saw him—three long years. Duke was the main reason behind that dreadful night and my current misery. So many feelings and thoughts ran across my mind as I stood there in the club, motionless.

Catching eye contact with him, I felt numb. It seemed as if Duke and I were the only two people standing there. I could feel his gaze as he slowly walked toward me.

Damn, he still looks good, I thought to myself. Duke was an excellent combination of Puerto Rican and black. With golden skin and hazel eyes, he was an automatic distraction. He smiled as he walked toward me. I couldn't walk or move. He was only two steps away from me when I heard yelling. Before I could turn and react to the noise, he grabbed my right hand and touched the left side of my face. I felt like I couldn't move. I was hypnotized by his presence. He spoke, and I didn't hear any words. I observed his handsome face and noticed a huge scar above his left eye. I didn't remember him having that scar, but I did remember the beatdown C gave him that night. We'd both left with physical scars that evening. He took his hand from my face, which brought me back to focus.

"Hey, Duke," was all that could escape my lips. I couldn't believe Duke had this effect on me. I thought seeing him would bring rage, anger, and fury, but I felt the total opposite.

The yelling behind me became louder, and more people were running to the racket. Turning around, I saw the same females Jaz had her incident with. They were throwing blows and stomps at the floor.

Shit, I thought. *Jaz!* I began to rush to the crowd. It was so crunk I had to literally hit a bitch to reach the situation. By the time I got to the center, the bitches fled, and Jaz was nowhere in sight. *She was on the floor before I got here*, I thought.

Just then, someone tapped my shoulder. When I turned around, I saw it was Jaz. Her face was red, and she was pissed.

"You okay?" I asked, looking her over.

Instead of words, her answer was punching me in the face. My head turned quickly after her strike. "You foul-ass bitch! How you let some shit like that go down?! You up here talking to a nigga, while I get jumped," she yelled. "The same nigga that's the reason yo' ass lonely now!"

I felt so ashamed, so humiliated. Hell, I'd barely said anything to

Duke. It didn't even seem like one minute had passed. I didn't come because I couldn't move, let alone hear. I knew Jaz was ready to straight brawl with me, but I wasn't ready. When she got amped up like this, it was so hard to calm her back down. Jaz was so damn crazy and wild. It was hard for her to walk away from bullshit and trouble. Of all nights, why couldn't this go smooth and drama-free?

From behind her, I could see the same two hood-rat bitches approaching. They returned with a couple more girls. They looked just as cheap and ghetto.

I warned Jaz. "Fuck all that. Them hoes back." At that point, I reached in my purse to get my blade. *Here we go again*, I thought. Jaz turned around knuckled up and ready to jack.

The crowd became rowdy as well as bigger as we stood face-to-face with our foes. The four of them were scared, and I could sense it. They thought we would run or back down, but nope … We were confident and ready.

Jaz retrieved her blades and stood tall at them bitches, for once not passing the first punch. Out of nowhere, Shay appeared, bare feet with both boots in hand. "What the fuck going on?! Fuck that shit," she screamed, hitting the female closest to her with a cowboy boot.

That initiated the scrap out. I caught a couple baby blows to the face before I laid the bitch competing with me completely out. The boxing lessons that C gave me eventually paid off in a long run. I was not the helpless girl who could not defend herself. I assisted Jaz by punching one of the two girls she was battling. Shay was going head-to-head with her opponent. We were getting the best of them.

The crowd reacted as we dropped them like flies. They fought like young schoolgirls, pulling hair and trying to scratch our faces up. As one of the chicks fell to the ground and got to vigorously shaking, security started yelling and heading over. We immediately fled the scene. We left out the back door with Will and his entourage. The stretch SUV was waiting out back for us. We all hopped in quickly, and the vehicle sped off just as quick.

Jaz and Marcus had somehow left together, leaving only Shay, Will, Ryan, and me. My face and hands were stinging. I could feel them swelling. I had blood on my arms and my blouse. It was silent in the limo. Well, besides the sound of Will and Shay making out.

The driver dropped off the affectionate couple first, and Shay promised to call me in the morning as she exited. Ryan and I were still quiet, and the car ride seemed awkward. I could only imagine what he thought of me now. Our night had been going so great. I enjoyed talking and flirting with him, and now I felt a bit embarrassed. We eventually pulled up to my house. Like the perfect gentleman, Ryan walked me to my front door.

"So ..." Ryan began, breaking the ice. "Are you going to take me up on that offer of dinner sometime, beautiful?"

I smiled at his attempt, and my jaw hurt for a minute. I grabbed my face and rubbed my jaw a little to soothe the pain. "Yes, I would love to."

"Great. I really enjoyed my night with you, Sydney."

"Likewise."

We exchanged digits, and he told me he'd call tomorrow. We ended the night with a soft kiss on the cheek. I stepped in the house, and my back fell against the door. This night was wild yet fulfilling. I smiled as I thought about everything on the way to my bedroom. I stripped down and went to run a bubble bath. I appreciated hot, steamy, long baths. I could see the steam rising from the water as I stepped in.

Within my last three years of being a dedicated mother and celibate, I'd learned to embrace my alone time. It was a time for me to manifest my own thoughts and appreciate the little things in life. Yet, I couldn't take my mind off Ryan. I could picture him as I sat in the hot water. My thoughts became more sexual as I bathed my body. I could imagine Ryan's hands replacing my loofah, which I was using to slowly wash my breasts.

I felt horny. I felt aroused. I began to touch my body. I ran my fingers over my breasts, then my stomach, and then down to my pussy. I softly rubbed myself as I sat in the hot, sweltering water. I used my fingers to spread my pussy open. I slid two fingers inside my wetness. I opened my legs wider as I leaned back against the tub. I laid my head against my bath pillow. I thought about Ryan touching me, about Ryan fucking me. My thoughts and my fingers had me climaxing in minutes. I couldn't believe I was feeling this, wanting him.

I had been celibate since the incident, and it had been a long time since I'd lusted for a man. I finished my bath, dried off, and oiled my body. I slipped in C's old T-shirt. I got comfortable in my plush bed, and before my mind could endlessly wonder, I fell asleep.

CHAPTER 2

Shit. The loud ringing from the telephone broke my sleep. I turned over in bed and stared up at the vaulted ceiling while the phone rang. It was a Saturday morning. I had an entire day planned with my baby girl. Time with my daughter was always appreciated, and I looked forward to my weekends with her. We always had so much fun together visiting unfamiliar places and creating new memories.

The ringing stopped. I sat up in bed and looked at the sunrays piercing through the window. I sat in my king-sized bed and glanced around my bedroom. My daughter had left several toys on the floor the night before. I got out the bed and walked across the room to the bathroom to take a shower. A hot shower always calmed me in the morning. I stepped out of the shower and decided to skip the gym today. Luckily for me, a trip to the gym was a walk down to my basement. I also enjoyed boxing and lifting, and my physique would suggest such.

As I dried off my six-foot, six-inch frame, I could hear my television being turned on. I then heard cartoon characters. I slid into my briefs and stepped into a pair of joggers before exiting the bathroom. There she was, sitting at the end of my bed. She was beautiful, just like her mother, although she still had my dominant features. She had my deep-brown complexion, lips, nose, and height. She was beautifully blessed with her mother's brown eyes and brown curly hair and had the shape of my round eyes.

"Good morning, my love," I greeted.

"Hey, Daddy," she happily replied. "Come on." She waved for me to come watch her favorite show with her. She sang the theme song, as I sat on the floor. She kissed me on the top of my head once I sat. She was affectionate like her mother. I adored that. We watched one episode, and she began to jump up and down in the king-sized bed. The commercials began to roll, and she giggled with glee.

"Okay, baby, let's get you in the tub and changed so we can go get breakfast," I told her as I stood up.

"Yes! Yay! Okay, Daddy," she yelled as she continued to jump.

"Come on," I told her with my arms open.

She fearlessly jumped into them. With her in my arms, I headed to her bedroom. I gave her a quick bath and set out a new pink floral dress.

"I can pick my own shoes, Daddy," she confidently told me.

"Okay, baby, finish getting dressed. I'll be back," I told her. I walked into my vast closet to put on something casual. I could hear the phone ring as I put on my loafers. I ran to the phone before they could hang up and greeted, "C."

"You still answer your phone like that?" Shorty joked on the other end.

I smiled at the sound of her voice. "Yep, it won't change. Sup?"

"Oh, nothing. Were you bringing her home today?"

"No. We may swing by, but I'll keep her for the rest of the weekend."

"Okay, that's fine. Tell her I love her."

"Okay."

Our conversation ended. I headed downstairs and out the front door. Cupcake was walking to my black, 1998 GMC Denali. She looked adorable in her pink dress and matching headband. She had picked silver sandals with pink bows.

"Which one, Daddy?" she asked, standing in the driveway.

My SUV and luxury whip were the only cars not in the garage. I owned a few whips.

"We're taking this one," I told her as I began walking toward the black-on-black 1998 BMW 750LI. "Your mom said she love you," I stated, opening the door for my princess.

"Daddy, I want to sit in the front with you. I'm a big girl now," she declared, reaching for the passenger handle.

"Okay then, lil Shorty. Just this one time. Then you got to get in your car seat," I said, meaning it.

She had that bossy and sassy attitude at times, just like her mother. She chatted about anything and everything on our way to her favorite pancake shop. We arrived shortly after, and based on the parking lot, it didn't appear crowded. Cupcake practically skipped to the building. The hostess sat us at a small table near a window and gave us complimentary orange juice.

We could see the fountain outside. Cupcake's face lit up as she watched the birds bathe in the water. "Dad, I know exactly what I want," Cupcake stated, sipping her orange juice.

The waitress came, and I quickly ordered our meals. Cupcake continued to talk her little face off. I looked around the restaurant and noticed a familiar face. It was Shorty's friend Shay. As usual, every time I saw her, she was with a different guy. She saw me and politely waved, revealing a well-manicured hand and fingers covered in diamonds. It surprised me that was still alive and still had no kids. She still looked good, though.

"Hey, Shay," Cupcake abruptly yelled across the room, waving.

"Sh, quit hollering," I advised.

Shay waved back with a smile. I remembered when Shorty first met Shay. I took her shopping on the strip, and Christian was working in the most expensive shoe store. She and Shorty instantly clicked when they met. Shay was older and knowledgeable about all the latest fashions and how to accentuate the body. In a sense, Shorty looked up to her. She was independently established, and overall, she was cool. I was aware of her promiscuous lifestyle, but that didn't stop the friendship her and Shorty founded.

The waiter then brought our hot breakfast. We devoured our food and washed up before heading out the door. The mall was only five miles away, so we were there in minutes. Cupcake ran to the first store that sold toys once we entered the mall. I humbly followed, as my cell phone began to ring.

"C," I greeted.

"Wut's up, nigga," my homeboy Trail hollered on the other end.

Trail was my ace. He was once my plug when I first got in the dope game. I jumped off the porch early, and Trail was there to mold me. I grew up watching him. Even though he was my mentor, I considered him a brother.

"What's happening?" I replied, following Cupcake through the store.

"Aye, you know Wiz throwing a house party tonight."

Wiz was my homeboy from grade school and the hood. He stayed a couple doors down from me in the hood. We pretty much jumped off the porch together. I graduated the dope game and college. Wiz took a different path. He was always a ladies' man, so he made a career of it.

"Yeah, I think I remember him mentioning that on the court the other day," I stated.

"Yeah, well, pregame at my crib, homie," Trail invited.

"A'ight bet."

Our conversation ended. Cupcake and I stopped in a few more stores, and I even window-shopped for Shorty's upcoming twenty-seventh birthday in a couple of months. After spending a few hundred in a few hours, we headed out. I decided to stop by Shorty's house first since I had plans to go out now. I had to use her spare key once I arrived because she didn't answer the door or the phone. I knew she was inside because her car was in the driveway. She could have been asleep, in the tub, masturbating, or in the tub masturbating.

Once inside, I could hear her screaming from the back that she was in the tub. I knew her. I shook my head with a smile as I took a seat on her sofa. Cupcake immediately ran to the back to see her mother and show off some of her new things. My thoughts then drifted to walking back to see Shorty in the tub. My Shorty, naked, wet ... in the tub.

My thoughts were then interrupted by the ring of the telephone. Thinking I was home, I picked up, "C."

"Hello?" they questioned on the other end. It was a man. "Hello," they blurted again.

"Yeah," I said.

"Sydney there?" he questioned with authority.

"She busy."

"Busy? Who is this?" he anxiously inquired. I knew what I was saying was uncalled for, but I didn't like the tone of his voice.

"Is this her baby daddy?" he stated.

"That's mighty disrespectful," I declared with a grin.

"Yeah, she told me about you. You're *just* her baby daddy. You sure she busy, bro?"

I knew right then and there that I did not like this person. "You want to leave a message, homie? She busy," I told him again. I knew that would aggravate him.

"I'll just call back when you not there," he stated and hung up the phone.

"Yeah, she found a real bitch nigga," I mumbled as I hung up the receiver. When I looked up, Shorty was standing right there. She wore only a soft blue towel and drops of water. She was just furiously looking at me with her hands on her perfectly shaped hips. She had a sexy look that I adored when she got angry. I also knew with that look came the bitching.

"Who was that?" she asked, looking so sexy to me.

I just shrugged my shoulders. Truthfully, I didn't know. He did all that questioning and never left his name.

"You were just having a conversation with someone and don't know their name?" she stated.

"I'm not sure. Some dude," I replied.

The phone rang again. She rushed over to answer it. I reached to answer, and she demanded, "Don't answer my phone!"

I chilled back on the couch. I figured it was that dude because I could hear her questioning him about what was said. She hung up and then looked at me. "What the fuck is your problem, C?! You cannot come over here answering my phone like you at home," she yelled at me.

I just looked at her. She knew I wasn't the malicious type. That guy was an asshole. Her face appeared a bit swollen, and her right hand was wrapped in bandages. I could tell she probably had some personal issues going on that had nothing to do with this. She was angry and ready to take her wrath out on anyone. Her negative energy was not wanted, so I said nothing.

"Do you hear me?! You are not my man anymore, C," she remarked loudly.

Damn. For some reason, that really hurt. I knew it'd been three years since we'd broken up and she initially hurt me, but hearing her say it … It hurt. I wasn't and guess I could never be her man again.

"A'ight, Shorty," I complied, standing up. "Come on, baby girl," I yelled for my daughter. I abruptly left, and for some weird reason, I was now angry—maybe jealous. I wasn't sure, but I was in a mood. That's the thing with energy. It travels so easily. I didn't want my baby to ride along with me with this vibe, so I decided to drop her off at my older sister Vicki's house. She enjoyed it over there. Vicki was my oldest sister by four years and my only sibling. She was happily married with three children, and Cupcake always had fun there. I dropped her off and promised I would be back in the morning to pick her up. I took a quick trip home to hit my gym and work off some stress. I worked out for 90 minutes straight. It always eased my mind and nerves. Exercising balanced my energy. I took a nice hot shower and lay across the bed thinking about the encounter at Shorty's house. Shortly after, I was asleep.

I awoke hours later, feeling refreshed. Fresh kicks, blue jeans, and a fly T was the attire for the house party. I brushed my low waves and put on my twenty-four-karat gold herringbone and a gold Rolex to compliment before I left my bedroom. I headed over to Trail's. I pulled up to Trail's half an hour later. Trail still lived near the hood we were from. Of course, I had moved farther away. I had a family to raise. Trail still loved the hood, and the hood still loved Trail.

We got fucked up at Trail's crib. We smoked a few blunts, took a few shots, and talked a lot of shit before we headed out. Wiz always threw the crunkest house parties. He would rent out huge houses in upscale neighborhoods and throw straight hood parties. He would bring all the dope niggas and going hoes out. And, of course, he had his girls on deck. I never left lonely if I didn't want to. Wiz had the whole block on swole when we arrived.

We went in, hollered at Wiz, and then posted up at the bar. We then saw Shay walking across the room with yet a different man from earlier today.

"Aye, aye, ain't that Shorty's friend?" Trail asked me as she made her way through the room.

"Yeah, that's Shay," I answered him, not focused on her anymore.

"Damn! She fine and stout! I don't remember her looking that damn good! I want her, C!"

All I could do was laugh. Listening to Shorty all the time, Shay wanted someone with endless funds. Now, I'm not saying Trail isn't financially successful. However, Trail ain't no trick. Trail is a street nigga. He's street smart as well as book smart. He was the person who schooled me on the legit ways get money. He showed me the ropes in the dope game. He taught me how to cook, flip and eyeball dope. As well as how to invest and profit off my funds. He pushed for me to leave the hood and go to college. He even had me going to trade schools to get a few trades under my belt. He funded the whole thing.

Trail was a huge investor when I had the idea to open my construction company with Duke once we graduated. I could see him building up the courage to go talk to her, even though she was with her man. Trail was shorter than me and a few shades lighter. Our builds were completely different' he was smaller. He didn't have a low cut, more like a small afro.

"I'm 'bout to go talk to her," he told me proudly.

"Good luck," I joked as he walked away. I laughed at the thought of them as he went to approach her. The guy she was with wasn't near her. Wow, he just might have a chance. They were now having a conversation. I turned to the bartender to order another shot of cognac. I quickly took the shot and turned around to peep the scene. There were a few people there I knew—homies from the hood and a few chicks I smashed in the past.

Then, taking a double look, I saw Duke. The same nigga who fucked Shorty—the only other person besides myself, as a matter of fact. It had been years since I'd seen him. I hadn't seen him since I beat him unconscious and had him liquidate and turn his shares of our used-to-be company over to me. After all the physical damage and court drama from that disaster of a night, I thought he skipped town for good. I figured he moved back home. He was talking to some guy, and I saw that he noticed me. My old friend, business partner, college buddy, now foe, and enemy. He nodded his head at me, and I could see him starting to walk my way.

What could we possibly have to talk about? I thought as he obviously made his way to me. I would've killed him if I never got that phone call about Shorty. Before I knew it, he stood before me.

"What's up, C?" he greeted.

I just looked at him. *Really, nigga?* I noticed the scar on his face where I pistol slapped him. That made me smile.

"How you been? I saw Shorty last night—"

Before I knew it, my fist hit his face. It was a mouth shot. I heard *Shorty*, and all my rage came from out of nowhere. That woman hurt me deeply. It caught him off guard too, as he fell backward, over a couch, and onto the floor. The DJ stopped the music.

Damn, I thought, as I saw his body lying there unresponsive. I didn't mean to start anything at my homeboy party. I didn't want no bullshit, but he should've never approached me. I don't care that three years has passed. We have nothing to rap about. I threw my hands up in a gesture to say my bad, as I could see Wiz from the other side. He was smoking a blunt, surrounded by a group of his girls.

He mimicked my gesture and yelled, "DJ, bring that shit back!" The DJ dropped the beat, and the party continued to go on. I looked back and saw that a couple of guys were carrying Duke out the door.

The music was pumping, and the party was jumping. I went to the dance floor and hopped behind the first big bouncing booty I saw. I was hoping she was fine because she could sure move her ass.

She turned around and her face said, "Run!"

I politely smiled, thanked her for the dance, and walked away. I then glanced the room to hopefully find me a nightcap. I wanted some head now. I saw a tall, sexy chick standing along the wall and decided to get her. It was never hard for me to get a woman. I spit my game, and moments later, we were behind the club in my SUV with my dick down her throat. She sucked a good dick. She took her time. I didn't feel much of her teeth. But no one compared to Shorty. I trained her well on how to satisfy me with her mouth and lips. Just thinking about her head made me come faster with this chick. She wanted to fuck, but I declined. I got what I wanted. I gave her one of my numbers on a hundred-dollar bill and told her to call me. I figured I could keep her around for distinct purposes since I just dropped a chick for becoming clingy.

It wasn't too late, so I stopped by Vicki's to get Cupcake. The ride home was silent since she was asleep, and the radio was off. We made it home, and I let her sleep in the bed with me. We snuggled and drifted off.

CHAPTER 3

A week had passed since I'd seen or heard from C. He dropped Cupcake off with a hello and goodbye. I could feel his energy was off when he did. Maybe he was upset over that small quarrel last week, even though I felt that wasn't enough for him to avoid me.

I cherished the strong friendship we developed after our split. I wanted to call and at least ask why he was being so distant, but my pride wouldn't allow me. Hell, my pride was what was keeping me from C. To date, I had never apologized for cheating on him. He never deserved what I did to him. We'd never really talked about it—never seemed to have the time. After the scandalous sex with Duke, then the almost-fatal car accident, I was hospitalized for weeks. We kind of just separated.

I now understood the embarrassment and distrust I caused that man. I was truly sorry. However, I could never own up to say those words to him. An apology would never reduce the pain or anger I caused him. I knew he probably needed to hear it, but I felt I had lost him, so what was the point. I couldn't let myself get wrapped up in C. We were not together. *I should not let our vibrational static bother me*, I thought.

I then began to think about Ryan. We had been on two dates since we'd met, and we were growing closer. It was an early Saturday afternoon, and I didn't have anything planned to do. Cupcake was over her aunt Vicki's house, and I couldn't find Shay or Jaz. I tried to call them, but neither were home.

I knew Jaz was on a hunt to find Marcus. When I last talked to her, she saw a videotape that Marcus secretly recorded of them having drunken, wild sex the night they met. I could not believe it when she told me. Once I saw the tape, I understood her vendetta. Now she was on a mission to find Marcus. She was crazy. Sometimes I wondered how I could be friends with someone so dangerous, but she had been my homegirl since high school. Jaz had a very caring spirit, but in the same breath, she could breathe fire.

Shay, on the other hand, seemed to be falling for Trail. She went on and on when she told me about him. I was totally shocked. But she said she liked him because he had a backbone and was different from most men she'd dated.

I stretched out on my plush sofa and decided to take a nap. Before I could get comfortable, I heard a car pull up. I looked out the window to observe Shay getting out of an older model compact car with an unattractive man. I unlocked the doors as she headed up the walk way.

She entered and spoke. "What's up girl?"

She was dressed casually, in stonewashed blue jeans, a white button shirt that she tied up in the front, and a pair of Doc Martens.

"Hey," I greeted as she took a seat. "I don't mean no harm, but who was that ugly-ass dude?"

"Girl, that's Eric," she said as if I should know him.

"What does he do?"

"He works at Auto Zone."

"He owns an AutoZone," I joked to see if she was playing. Shay had never dated a guy of that status.

"Girl, he is essential! He can fix shit, he works hard to please me, and he got a food stamp credit card thing," she told me with a laugh.

"Lord, Shay," I huffed. I laughed at her meaning of needing him. Her idea of a man's necessities was more like accessories.

"Have you heard from Jaz?" she asked.

"No, you know she is looking for Marcus."

"Yeah, I almost forgot," she responded.

My telephone then rang. "Hello, my Sydney," a voice said into the receiver. I quickly recognized the voice as Ryan's. He always called, every day. I liked that. He wasn't shy about his interest in me. It made me feel wanted again.

"Hello to you," I happily said back.

"Would you like some company?"

"Got some."

"Who?" he spit back with a sense of jealously.

I immediately felt a bit aroused from his increased emotion. "Oh, it's just Shay," I told him.

Shay looked over with a playful eyeroll.

"Oh, okay. So how is your girl Jaz doing? I saw the videotape," he instigated, with a small laugh.

"That's not funny. Don't let Jaz hear you laughing like that."

"I don't care either way. He's just a coworker. But what she gonna do, kill me?" he jokingly asked.

"You think she's incapable?" I replied with a grin.

"Well, I'm on my way over if that's cool with you...?"

"That's cool. I'll be here," I responded to him and then hung up the phone.

"That was Ryan, huh?" Shay quoted, exiting the kitchen with a big bowl of grapes.

"Yes, it was. He's on his way over," I announced with glee.

"You plan on dropping them panties for him too, huh?" she quizzed with curiosity in her eyes.

"Hell yes," I wanted to answer but didn't. Instead, I told her nonchalantly, "I don't know. Maybe."

It had only been a week since Ryan and I started dating, but I also knew I liked him. He was a gentleman, he was thoughtful, and he was open about how he felt. I was never exposed to that. I was very private with my emotions because I was raised like that. My mother passed away when I was too young to remember. The only relationship I'd ever had was with C, and he was very prideful. It was refreshing to have a man who openly expressed his thoughts and feelings.

Many thoughts and a half hour later, Ryan was knocking at my door. I opened the door, and there stood the handsome Ryan. He greeted me with a warm hug and soft kiss on the cheek. Ryan was very understanding that I wanted to take things slow. I appreciated that about him. We then snuggled up on the couch together, while Shay lounged on the recliner. She channel surfed until she found an action/comedy movie to watch.

"Where is Will?" Ryan asked Shay.

She humped her shoulders in response. We were all enjoying the movie, and I was enjoying being in Ryan's arms. I was also enjoying the soft kisses he was placing on the back of my neck. I don't think he understood how that little motion was turning me on big time. His lips against my skin felt lovely. I wanted him so bad. Three years was a long time to go without the touch or comfort of a man. I could feel a slight sensation in my lower groin as his big arms were wrapped around me and his warm breath and soft lips kissed my skin. I could feel myself becoming moist. *Wow.* I turned around to face him and asked, "Why are you doing that?" I was smiling, and a part of me didn't want him to stop.

He smiled back and said, "My apologies. You're just so irresistible." He then kissed my face. The light touch of his facial hair against my cheek made me feel vulnerable in his arms.

Before I could give in and kiss him, my doorbell rang. Thank heavens—saved by the bell. Shay answered, and it was Jaz. Jaz immediately came in, spoke to Ryan, and ordered Shay and I to the back. We obliged and followed her. She closed the door and pulled out a videocassette as we gathered in my bedroom.

I figured she must've forgotten she'd showed us this already. "Jaz, you know we seen this, right?"

"Not this one," she stated with an evil grin as she popped it in the VCR.

The tape came on, and the camera moved erratically at first. Then you could see a man, Marcus probably. He was dressed like a woman, in makeup and a wig, and crying. He appeared to be hog-tied to a wooden dining chair.

While in tears, you could hear him repeating over and over, "I'm a bitch. I'm a pussy."

You could also hear a woman, possibly Jaz, in the background laughing and giving directions. She fast-forwarded through minutes of torture and his cries. She then paused and pressed play. "You ready?" is all you could hear, and then the video ended. Just like that.

Jaz laughed hysterically as Shay and I looked at each other awkwardly. I didn't know what to say. I could only be thankful that she was a friend and not an enemy.

"So y'all liked it?" she squeaked as she ejected the tape.

We both nodded in agreement and in fear. This was like the third person she has kidnapped—that we knew of. Even more odd was the fact that she never faced any judicial repercussions. I always wondered how she could get away with so much, but frankly, I was too afraid to ask. I accepted my friend for whoever and whatever she was.

"Sydney, what are you doing?" Ryan yelled from upfront.

"I'm about to go kick it with Ryan," I told them as I got up to exit.

"That's cool. I might just go give his homeboys a copy," Jaz stated as she got up to follow me out of the room.

"We going to the club later. You rolling, Jaz? I got us VIP," Shay offered.

"Yeah. I'll meet back up with you guys later," Jaz told us and then left.

We began to chill back on the sofas. Shay turned to the music video channel for us to watch the latest videos. I was back in Ryan's arms. I was about to drift off before some random guy came to pick up Shay. She promised she would call and come back later. Ryan and I were cuddled up and eventually fell asleep.

I awoke at least an hour later, and Ryan was gone. I couldn't believe he left me without waking me up. I wondered if maybe he realized I didn't have on any makeup. Maybe he saw the scars. I had easily become so comfortable with him that I'd forgotten to cover my mutilations. I sat up on the sofa and began to hear noise from the kitchen. I hopped up to see what it was, and there was Ryan. He hadn't left me. I smiled.

"What you got to eat?" he asked, rambling through my kitchen cabinets.

"If you're that hungry, I can cook you something," I informed, walking over to him.

"Okay, that's cool," he said, closing the cabinet doors.

I instructed him to leave the kitchen and head to the sofa, so I could prepare him a quick, hot meal. I pan-fried a few pieces of chicken breast and decided to make pasta and vegetables on the side. Shortly after, we were at the dining table eating. Ryan ate as if he hadn't in weeks. I was happy he enjoyed my food. That was always my favorite part of cooking—other people enjoying it.

We conversed over dinner and wine. Ryan really opened up to me at my dining table. He told me about his dark childhood. He was in the foster system. He'd never really had anything, not even a family. That's why he was so appreciative of everything. He told me about all the horror stories he experienced growing up in the system.

We spoke about past relationships and how important trust was. Trust. That was a sensitive subject for me. Knowing my past deception and hearing he was recently cheated on, I was happy when my telephone rang.

"Hello," I greeted.

"Hey, princess," said the most important man in my life—my father.

"Hey, Daddy," I replied in a tone of teen girl. I loved my Daddy. He was the only family I had besides my daughter. My dad had a lucrative real estate company where I worked full time. I was once one of his top-selling agents, but after the accident, I stepped back from the spotlight.

"Hey, Shorty," I could hear Daphne scream in the background. Daphne was the love of my dad's life. They had been together for years, although they weren't married. My dad was still a widow from the death of my mother.

"Tell her I said hello," I replied.

"How are you today?" he asked.

"I'm great, Dad. Cupcake's gone, so I was enjoying dinner with a friend," I told him.

He could hear a male's voice in the background. "Oh, C over there?" he asked.

"No. Ryan," I responded. I then realized I hadn't told my father about Ryan yet.

"Ryan? I haven't heard about this Ryan," he declared on the other end.

"I know, Dad. It's nothing too serious," I responded to him.

My dad kept me on the phone for another thirty minutes, telling me about an upcoming jazz show he and Daphne planned to attend. We ended our conversation with I love yous and hung up the receivers. Ryan left shortly after. I decided to take a long, hot bubble bath and get ready for my night out later. As I sat at my vanity table, my telephone rang.

"Hello," I greeted.

"Hey, girl," Shay said back happily.

I could hear excitement and enthusiasm in her voice. *Someone must've bought her a new car*, I thought. But, no. She was tickled pink that Trail told her no.

"Yes, girl! I asked him to rent a limo and order VIP for all of us at the club right, and he straight up told me, 'Who the fuck do you think I am?!' Oh my gosh he sounded so sexy," she gushed.

"I thought you didn't like when guys told you no," I asked her.

"Exactly. It's like so bold for him to tell me no. It's something about him," she replied. Her line then buzzed. "Hold on," she told me and clicked over.

I was wondering if had Shay finally met her match. She then clicked back over. "Yeah, that was Lewis. We'll be over in a couple hours to pick you up. If you talk to Jaz, tell her to meet us at All Night. It's jersey night, so you know all the ballers gonna be out," she stated before getting off the phone.

I then called Jaz. She wasn't home, so I left a message on her answering machine. I put on some high-waisted, tight, white Calvin Klein jeans and a brightly colored, cleavage-revealing crop top. I swooped my bangs and pulled by hair away from my face. I put on some makeup, matching the bright colors of my top to my eye shadow. I slipped on some wedge-heel, multicolor sandals to show my beautiful, pedicured toes.

Shay arrived in my driveway almost two hours later. I hopped in the limo with her and her date for the night. Shay wore a revealing, tight, long skirt with long slits up her hips. You could see her paw-print tattoos going up her thigh. She paired it with a black-and-gold silk Versace top.

Of course, we opened a bottle of Cristal, and by the time we reached the nightclub, the bottle was empty. We pulled up, and it was packed. Tonight, was jersey night. All the fellas had on their favorite team's jersey.

All Night wasn't as prestigious as Silhouette, but I enjoyed the vibe there. It felt good receiving the attention we got as we walked through the doors of the club. Several guys tried to hit on me, before we reached VIP. I declined all offers. I was fixated on meeting Ryan that night. I loved when he saw me all made up and dressed up. I felt the most confident.

Surprisingly, VIP was just as crunk. That was rare. I could feel my anxiety increasing as the hostess led us through the crowed room to our booth. I didn't like this scene. It was too many people. Half an hour and a couple double shots later, Ryan still hadn't arrived. I was irritated. I wanted to leave, so I decided to go out on the dance floor. Shay didn't want to join, so I danced to a couple songs by myself.

After I worked up a small sweat, I decided to take a seat at the main bar and ordered a water. Some unattractive guy offered to buy me a drink, and I declined. I moved down a stool to ensure he wouldn't try to converse with me again as I drank my ice water.

The fellow next to me smelled so scrumptious. He wore a very familiar scent, Armani mixed with marijuana. That scent could easily get me aroused. I turned to see, but his back was facing me. *Damn.* Even his back was sexy. He had sexy, broad shoulders with a huge, tall frame. I loved a man with big shoulders. He was so statuesque. I wanted to see his face, but all I could see was the baseball cap that he had turned backward. He had on the matching baseball jersey and some baggy blue jeans. I turned back to face the bar and order another glass of champagne. Moments later, Mr. Baseball Cap turned around. Turning to meet his eye contact, I saw it was C.

I looked him over, and I could feel him doing the same. It was obvious he had been working out more because I could see the definition through his tank top. He wore his baseball jersey open, showing his white tank, which hugged every muscle in his torso. He stared at me as if he had never seen me before.

"Hey, C," I greeted as I turned my barstool completely toward him.

"Shorty. What's up?" he spit back, looking oh so sexy.

He showed a slight smile, and it made my pussy smile. C always had a beautiful, bright smile for me. His low-cut beard only complimented his ravishing bone structure.

"How have you been?" I asked, curious to know. It had been a week since we'd talked.

"Good. And you?"

"I've been well. You're the last person I thought I'd run into here."

"Oh, really? I could say the same thing to you," he stated, nodding his head with a grin. "I see Shay finally got you going out every weekend," he joked.

"Something like that," I responded playfully. God, I missed C.

The bar became more crowded, and C was being pushed closer to me. He was practically between my legs and looking down at me. I looked up to him, and his fragrance made me want him bad. I then began to wonder if he was here with another woman. Maybe she was waiting in the cut, watching us flirt.

He interrupted my thoughts with his words, "You look really good tonight, Shorty."

I blushed. It felt good to hear him say that. I always appreciated his compliments. I stood up, so he could admire my outfit in its entirety. I confidently turned so he could see my dangerous curves and told him, "Thank you."

He really did look sexy tonight. I loved the thug side of C, as well as his corporate side. I treasured how he could wear an Armani suit with Louis Vuitton dress shoes or switch up in a Karl Kani baggy jean set with some Timbs or J's. I loved the versatility of C—something about a roughneck. I could feel my bubbly kicking in as I stood up from the barstool. There was a long pause. I wanted to ask who he came with, but a familiar love song pumped through the speakers. It was one our songs from our favorite male group, Jodeci. Many moons ago, we kissed for the first time to that song.

CHAPTER 4

Shit. It's our song. Shorty and I shared so many memories with that song. We shared remembrances with that whole album. We would always listen to music together, discovering new artists. We would sit in my car for hours, listening to all genres and talking about whatever. I can recollect when I first made love to her. That song played in the background as I took my time with her. I noticed the look on her face. I knew she could remember all the great times as well. We would dance together each time we heard the melodic voice of the male group.

The crowd continued to push us closer together. Her breasts were now pressed against me. There was no reason to break tradition, so I asked, "You want to dance?"

She paused and then answered, "Yes, I would love to."

I softly grabbed her hand and led her to the dance floor with me. We got on the floor, and I placed my hands on her delicate body. I lightly gripped her small waist and pulled her closer to me. She smelled delicious, like a pastry. Her eyes appeared to be a bit glossy. I knew she was probably inebriated. She was looking so high and sexy. I decide to flirt with her.

"You in the club trying to give my pussy away, huh?" I joked, looking at her in those light brown eyes.

Her eyes bucked as she laughed and answered, "C! Stop playing! I'm just here to have an enjoyable time." Her full lips looked inviting as she continued to smile at me.

"I know I've been gone too long. Your friends have turned you into a club hopper," I said.

"Oh no! It's nothing like that. I've just been enjoying getting dressed up and having fun," she told me.

Our song was coming to an end as I noticed some guy approaching us. He was dressed in all black, so I assumed he was a server or bartender. I looked at him and ordered, "Two shots of cognac."

He smirked at me. Shorty didn't see him until he announced, "Sydney!"

The music was loud, but I could hear the jurisdiction in the way he said her name—her government name, at that.

She turned and smiled at him. "Ryan," she shouted, releasing her arms from around my neck and jumping into his arms. She turned back around to introduce us. He was introduced as her friend, but I wasn't slow. I could tell he wanted to be her new man.

"Let's go back to VIP," he suggested to her.

"Okay. Thanks for the dance, C," she abided.

Ryan placed his hand on the small of her back, and they vanished into the crowd. I stood on the dance floor a few more minutes, tripping off what just happened. I started to make my way to the VIP as well. I needed that shot that Ryan didn't retrieve. I went to the bar.

The bartender immediately came to take my order, "What'd you have?"

I smiled and ordered, "You know ... I want a double shot of cognac. And let me get the whole bar too." Yep, I decided to buy the bar.

"That's $4,500," the bartender informed me.

"How do you want it?" I asked. I pulled a bankroll wrapped in rubber bands out of my Girbaud jeans. The crowd went wild around me as I dropped a few bands, and we all took a shot. The bartender jotted down my information and passed it to one of the sexy servers. I saw her beeline her way through the club to hand the info to the DJ.

Moments later, the DJ scratched the record and gave me the necessary shout out. "Aye yo! Aye yo! Shout out to Shorty's baby daddy for buying the bar tonight! Everybody in the club getting tipsy tonight, yo!" He then dropped the hottest rap track, and the club went bananas.

I looked over to observe a reaction from Shorty and her lame. I saw a brief smile on Shorty's face. I could easily see frustration on his. Shay was in the booth with them, and I could hear her laughing. She knew what was going on.

Immediately after, the club owner approached me. "C! It's C, right? Anyway, come on. Follow me. I got you a booth and everything," he quickly spoke. He talked and walked so fast I could barely keep up through the crowd.

Once I arrived at the booth, he had security instructing a group of fine-ass women away. The owner was giving idle promises to make the ladies relocate, although one woman refused to leave. She had a cute heart-shaped face and dark, deep-set eyes. She was boiling. I admired the look she had being mad.

"I'm not moving! I paid for this booth! I knew I should not have come out tonight! I knew we shouldn't have come to this hood-ass club," she screamed at the owner and bouncer.

"Ladies, ladies, ladies, please. You don't have to go anywhere. I'm just trying to party with you all," I conveyed as I tried to calm the situation.

"And who the fuck are you?" the disgruntled beauty asked.

"Aren't you somebody baby daddy?" one of her chicks asked aloud.

"I'm C, and yes. Look, my ex is here with her new boyfriend, and I just wanted them to have a good night. Drinks on me," I said as I raised my shot glass to toast.

There were a couple aws from the chicks in the clique. We toasted, and I took a seat next to the beautiful-eyed woman. Her body was tight. I could see her curves in the red skintight dress she wore. Her red satin shoes were expensive. I could tell she had taste. The bold red was ravishing against her chocolate skin. Her hair was long, black, and thick. She looked at me, and I could feel her look through me. Her long, slender neck made her look regal. She was hypnotizing.

"Rosa," I said to her.

"My name is not Rosa! Who do you think you talking to?" she asked. Her voice was raspy.

I smiled and mimicked, "'I'm not giving up my seat!'"

She looked at me, and then her face softened. She burst out laughing.

"Okay, you get it. Rosa Parks, refusing to move," I joked. She had a beautiful smile. The red lipstick made her gap-toothed sneer perfectly imperfect.

"Okay, that was funny," she admitted.

"Thanks, I normally have a few good jokes a day."

"Oh really? Well aren't you just the comedian."

I smiled at her, and she smiled back. "I just love your cute lil gap-toothed smile," I confessed. She blushed, and I asked, "So, what's your name, Rosa?"

"Evelyn."

"Beautiful name for a beautiful woman."

"So, what does the *C* stand for?"

"Carleon. Carleon Stone."

She nodded. The DJ had the club jumping. The flow of free drinks had everyone in happy spirits. The unanimous ladies' anthem blasted through the speakers. Evelyn's entire crew stood up to drunkenly sing along. I paid more attention to Evelyn, however. I watched how she sat in her seat to grind to the music. I observed her demeanor and how she spoke. It was something about her—something that was alluring. Her crew began to encourage her and I to get up and dance. I stood up and extended my hand to dance with her. She accepted.

We were grooving and grinding to the loud music. I enjoyed the feel of her body against mine. She was probably about 5'8 with her stiletto heels. The music began to slow down, and I began to pull her closer to me.

"So is this a part of the plan to make your baby momma jealous?" she asked as she looked up to me.

"No. Not at all. There was never a strategy with that objective. I told you, I was just being nice."

She wrapped her arms around my neck, and I placed mine around her waist. "Hm … nice, considerate, and generous? Now I'm wondering why you two are not together anymore," she said with a smile.

"Let's just say I have no luck when it comes to love."

"I can understand that. I've been single for quite some time now. Usually the risk just isn't worth it."

We stepped slowly to the music. Her statement was true. Somehow, we both felt the exact same way. The risk of getting hurt was never worth it for a shot at love. I glanced over the room and didn't even realize Shorty and her lame had disappeared. I was enjoying my time with Evelyn and her crew. The song ended, and so did our dance.

"Ev, let's go! We hungry," one of her homegirls yelled over the music.

"Last call! Last call," the DJ shouted over the speakers.

It was winding down and about time for the club to close. People were leaving, and they were about to start turning on lights.

"Okay, okay. Let's roll," Evelyn suggested.

I could see that she was the leader of her crew. She seemed to call all the shots.

"Do you mind if I walk you to your car?" I offered as she and her girls were preparing to leave.

Evelyn looked at me as she reached for her purse and said, "Sure."

I was excited she agreed. Typically, I would be walking a chick to my car to stuff her mouth with my dick. But now I was escorting a woman to her car, anxious to ask her on a date. I grinned at my nervousness. We reached the parking lot, and her friends had to help hold up one homegirl. She could barely keep her balance. Evelyn pulled out her keys as we reached her white Mercedes Benz SUV.

"So, can I see you again?" I inquired.

She looked me up and down. "Uh, I'm sure you're the man in the hood, but I'd rather not be among your flock of women, Mr. Stone," she declined.

I released a small laugh. She was judging me. I could feel her glance over me, my stance, and my attire and appraise me. I was probably some local drug dealer with multiple women in her eyes. That was laughable.

"So, are you implying I'm a street nigga and a player?"

"In lesser words ... yes."

I chuckled and said, "Okay ... Please allow me to take you to dinner sometime. I know we didn't have enough time or the right environment to really get to know each other. However, I would love to see you again. I would love to know everything about you. Soak in your beauty."

Her face softened as she smiled. I could feel she was warming up a bit.

"Just give me the chance to prove you wrong," I offered.

She reached in her matching red satin purse to retrieve a pen and paper. She jotted her digits down and slid in her car. I was excited, smitten even. We waved, and she pulled off the lot. I walked to my car, passing up several drunk, loose women. I drove to the house and slowly pulled into the driveway. I sat in my car, high as hell, but I still rolled a blunt. I was enjoying the high I felt Evelyn gave me. It did something to me that she turned me down. I smoked until I passed out, right there in the car. It was one a hell of a night.

CHAPTER 5

I hated last night. Everything about last night was horrible. Ryan pissed me completely off. He couldn't stop speaking on C, inquiring all about our past relationship and my present feelings for him. I woke up feeling terrible. I'm sure I carried the energy from last night into this new day. I sat up in bed and played back every moment from last night.

My slow dance with C was the best thing all night. At that point, Ryan came, and everything went sour. Then C's ego bought the bar. That simple, petty move ate Ryan up. I know it was meant to be sarcastic. After that, he continued to question me. He left once he realized I was annoyed. I couldn't reveal my true feelings about C to him, or anyone for that matter. I was hoping to capture C's attention once Ryan left early. However, some beautiful, dark-skinned chick beat me to the punch. From there, I drank several glasses of champagne and continued to take shots.

I got so drunk last night. I threw up soon as I got home. I was intoxicated enough to call C and pour my heart out. I'm sure he would've laughed at my honesty, and I was smashed enough to laugh right along with him. My night ended with me in tears and hugging my pillow next to the toilet.

I shook off my sluggishness. Today Shay was hosting a blowout sale at her boutique. I promised her I would be there to support and help. I sat on the toilet ready to relieve my bladder and discovered I was on my period. *Could today get any worse?* I thought.

I ran a light bubble bath as I relaxed and cleansed my body. I exited the tub and slipped into some comfortable, ripped jeans and a university sweatshirt. I threw my hair in a ponytail and slipped on some white sneakers. I called Vicki to inform her I would come by once I left the boutique. I grabbed my tote filled with mini cupcakes and wine. I then proceeded out the door.

I arrived at the shop shortly after. I entered the store, and Shay already had customers browsing around. She was prancing around in a vintage Dior sheer black dress. I greeted her with a hug and kiss on the cheek.

"Hey, pumpkin," she stated, matching the kiss on the cheek.

"I got cupcakes and wine," I announced as I made my way to the back of the shop. I went to set down my purse and tote bag in her office.

Shay was giving directions and issuing orders when I came out to help set up the table. "I'm so glad you could make it. Jaz should be here any moment now," she told me, sipping her mimosa.

"Ugh, girl, I'm on. Last night was awful. I'm just … here," I told her.

"Yeah, last night was crazy. C a fool for that," she chuckled.

I rolled my eyes. Shay took her attention off me as she looked at the cops come through her glass doors. She laughed and said loudly, "I'm sure you gentlemen are in the wrong place of business."

"Sydney Inox," the taller officer stated.

My heart plummeted. I could barely acknowledge that I was the person of interest. Shay laughed and looked in my direction.

"Sydney Inox," he repeated with authority.

The store became quiet.

"Yes," is all I could mumble.

They approached me. Three gentlemen—two officers and one detective. "Ms. Inox, were you at the nightclub Silhouette a couple weeks ago around 1:30 a.m.?" he quizzed.

"Yeah." I remembered. I was recalling that night. That fight.

"Were you in an altercation with this young lady?" he asked, holding up a picture.

"Possibly," I spit back.

He then began to get his handcuffs. He reached for my hands and began to read me my Miranda rights. I couldn't hear anything. Everything was blurry. I could see Shay begin to panic. As they walked me outside, I saw Jaz walking up. This was unbelievable. I could hear

Shay hysterically trying to explain to Jaz what was happening. I couldn't feel or hear anything. They stuffed me in the back of the police car.

Jaz grabbed me and told me, "Shorty, I'm so sorry. Please don't worry about anything. Don't say anything until your lawyer is present. I'll get you out of this." She looked me in my eyes as she spoke.

I didn't know what to say. The officers pulled off as she continued to talk. I rode the entire ride downtown not knowing my charge. I felt like a criminal. They threw me in a room and questioned me for hours. I obeyed Jaz and said nothing. They were trying to charge me with involuntary manslaughter. Somehow, one of the chicks we got to scraping with last week died on her way to the hospital. I remember someone was having a seizure before we bounced, but I didn't know it resulted in her death. I didn't try to hurt anyone. I only fought to defend myself and my friend. I didn't even want to go out that night. How ironic—someone noticed me since my baby daddy bought the bar last night. In just a blink of an eye, life can change.

Seventy-two hours later, Jaz and her legal team pushed for a speedy trial. I faced up to nine years in prison, although Jaz assured me I had nothing to worry about along the way. I couldn't believe I endured three days in jail. Jaz and my father had really been by my side throughout this whole ordeal. Jaz took care of the legal, and Pops took care of the personal and my sweet Cupcake.

The trial came and went, and just like Jaz promised, I was acquitted. Jaz was at the gate waiting once I was released. I bear-hugged her. She hugged me back just as tight.

"Girl! Thank you! Thank you! I owe you my life," I protested once I released her from my grip. I couldn't stop hugging her.

"No, you good, Shorty. That was my fault. I should've never involved you in that mess in the first place. If anything, I'm sorry. I see now I need to think before I react off my emotions," she admitted.

That was new—to hear her say something so mature. I'd always had a tight relationship with Jazmine, but she'd always kept a private side about herself. It never affected our friendship. After her few years away, she became more isolated. I respected her privacy, and she understood my complexity. We had a bond.

We held hands as we walked to her SUV. I was anxious to see my daughter. My father told her I was out of town on a top-secret work project. I cherished him for that. I didn't want my daughter to know where her mother had been. He told C the same story, without all the top-secret mumbo jumbo. He didn't need to know either. She took me home, and I immediately took a long, hot bubble bath. It felt great to bathe myself without numerous other women watching.

As I began to relax, the tears began to fall. At first, I was unsure of my tears. But again, alone time makes you appreciate the little things. I cried because I could take a bath and not a shower. I could account for my own time. I could eat what I wanted, when I wanted. I could see my baby and sleep in my comfortable bed. I was grateful. I got out the tub, refreshed, and dressed myself. I put on a pair of blue jeans and a white crop top and wrapped a plaid button-up around my waist. I even put on a little makeup. I went into my living room, and surprisingly, Jaz was still there.

"I thought you would be gone," I stated, taking a seat on the couch.

She was watching some scary movie on television. "Unfortunately, I have nowhere to be right now," she told me.

"Jaz, seriously, I just want to thank you again for everything. I sincerely appreciate that. I don't know how you did it, but you did."

She smiled at me and said, "We don't ever have to talk about that again, Shorty. You know I got you."

I found myself invested in the horror film she was watching, and then my telephone rang. "Hello," I greeted.

"Well, hello to you! Where have you been? I've been calling and coming over. You've been hiding," I heard Ryan state from the other end.

I looked over to my answering machine. It blinked eighteen new messages. Although Ryan had pissed me off a few nights back, I was thrilled to hear his voice.

"Out of town. For work," I lied.

"Where?"

"Ryan, what difference does it make? How are you?" I asked, trying to get him off the subject. I did not want him to know about my brief incarceration.

"I've been fine. Did you enjoy your trip?"

"I did," lying again. My line then buzzed. "Hold on, Ryan," I stated and then clicked over. "Hello?"

"Great. You're home. That's where you belong," my father replied.

"Hold on, Daddy," I told him. "Hello, Ryan, I will call you back. This my daddy."

"Okay, don't have me waiting for shit, Sydney," he replied and then hung up.

I clicked back over to my father. "Hey, Daddy! I missed you so much!"

"Glad your home, Shorty," I heard Daphne yell in the background.

"I missed you too, baby," he declared. I could feel his love from over the phone. "Now please don't scare me like that again. Shorty. I love you too much to ever risk losing you."

"Believe me, Dad. You won't. I don't even want to see a club," I stated seriously.

He then began to express how much I meant to him, preaching about how I should think before I react. Of course, my deceased mother came up in his lengthy dialogue.

"Where is my Cupcake, Daddy?" I asked, ready to go get my daughter. I was ready to smother her tiny, adorable face with a million kisses.

"She's with C. I forgot to tell you."

I could feel the anxiety come over my body. "Daddy, I told you to keep her."

"Well, C called and wanted to spend time with her. I cannot tell him no. It's his child too, Shorty. Besides, she wanted to go with her father, and I can't stop that."

"Oh," I spit out.

"Well, I have to go. Just wanted to ensure you were home safe. We're headed to the jazz show! I will talk to you later, sweetie. I love you."

C had our child. I had to go over to his house to get my baby. I rarely went back to that place. I then contemplated if I should call him and ask him to drop her off. Then I realized that would make me look weak. I stood up and told Jaz I was going over C's house to get Cupcake. I asked her if she wanted to join, and she declined.

"I can do this. I can do this," I chanted as I walked to my car. I continued my chant almost the entire ride over there. I noticed my anxiety as I gripped the steering wheel. The pure presence of C could make me nervous or horny or both. He had always possessed that influence over me. Him and his energy just did something to me. I was now standing at the door and taking deep breaths as I rang his doorbell.

CHAPTER 6

Shit, I thought as I got up. I was interrupted on my fifty-third push-up when the doorbell rang. I had been working out for the last hour and had totally lost track of time. I got up off the floor and proceeded to walk up the stairs. I wondered who could be popping up at my crib.

The doorbell continued to ring as I climbed the stairs. I was hoping whoever it was hadn't awakened my daughter while she peacefully slept in the den. I played her out earlier with gardening, skating, and board games. She was completely pooped and fell asleep on the couch. I snuck downstairs to get in a quick workout, while she napped.

I made my way across my foyer and opened the door. It was Shorty. My Shorty, just as beautiful as ever.

"Hello, C," she greeted as she looked my body over.

I was only in briefs and a pair of running shoes. I remembered she would always tell me my shoulders and chest were her hugest turn-on. I could feel the admiration as I saw her bite her bottom lip.

"What's up, Shorty? Didn't know you were back in town. Just as I didn't know you were leaving town. But hey … Come on in," I replied.

"Yeah," she mumbled. She continued her gaze upon my chest.

I was perspiring from my workout. She soaked up every inch of my body with her eyes. I stepped back so she could enter. She walked past me as I inhaled her sweet scent. We locked eyes for a moment. In that instance, I thought I felt a vibe. She smiled and then walked away to look for Cupcake. She walked over to look into the empty living room and then treaded over to the den where she was napping.

I could see her face light up when she saw our daughter. I smiled, realizing I could feel how much she missed CC. I knew she wanted to wake her. She turned to me and looked so youthful and full of joy. There was something different about her. Her energy and aura were so bright today.

"So, I interrupted your workout, I see," she stated as she took a seat on the sofa. She kissed Cupcake on her head once she sat. She continued to look my body over as I walked into the room.

"Yeah, I was about to finish up anyway," I admitted as I made my pecs jump.

She crossed her legs, and I flashed a grin. "You trying to get sexy, huh?" she said.

She was obviously flirting. I liked that she was opening up again to me. Upon our separation, she would hold back so much of herself. I appreciated the fact that we could be on that level. I sometimes missed the relationship, the connection, we once shared. I wondered what would happen if we ever talked about what happened, how it happened, why it happened. It was crazy that we'd never spoken about it, but pride is a mutha fucker. Of course, it was a conversation that was long overdue. Yet, years had passed us by. The attempt to try to fix what was broken was futile.

"You tell me … Am I sexy?" I asked her, flexing.

"You know you are … not," she said, laughing.

I brushed her off with a laugh. "Whatever."

"No, but seriously. You are, C. Very sexy. Everything about you," she told me with a look in her eyes.

I dismissed myself to get some sweatpants and a tank. Shorty had me feeling … something. I felt like she was trying to seduce me with her words and her eyes. There was a sensation there, and it was working. I entered back into the den. The TV was muted, and Shorty was admiring our daughter. She ran her fingers through CC's curls while she slept. It was quiet.

Shorty's cell phone ringing broke the silence. She stood up, frantic as she listened to the call. I eavesdropped to try to understand what was going on. She became very edgy as she stood up to pace the floor. She started screaming into the phone, almost waking up our daughter. I immediately ran to her side and began to hold her. She closed her phone and ended the phone call. She started to cry in my arms. She sobbed hard as I wrapped my arms around her tighter. She then broke from my embrace.

"Shorty? Is everything okay?" I asked as she looked off into a distance.

"I gotta go, C," she announced, shaking her head.

"Shorty?! Shorty," I repeated as I attempted to catch her.

She hurried out the door without saying goodbye or even telling me what was going on. I stood in the doorway as she screeched out my driveway. That was so weird. Just when I thought Shorty was opening up, she was shutting me back out. I went back downstairs to stretch my body. I spent several minutes before and after any intense workout to complete proper stretching. After gulping an entire bottle of water, I stretched out onto the floor. I started to relax and fell asleep on the mat.

Half an hour later, I was awakened from Cupcake shoving me. "Dad, Daddy," she called as she poked at me to wake up.

I sat up on the floor and smiled at my daughter. I could feel the soreness in my body. "Hey, baby. I must've fell asleep after stretching," I reported. I stood up and looked over to my baby. She was sitting on my bench press.

"Daddy, when you done exercising, can we go to the park," Cupcake asked, legs swinging.

"It's getting dark out, baby girl. How about we go to One Stop where we can grab a bite to eat and play a few games," I suggested.

Her face lit up. "Yes! Okay, Daddy," she exclaimed as she hopped up. "I'm going to put my shoes on," she gushed before running upstairs.

"Okay, okay. I have to take a shower first, baby," I informed her. I followed behind her and headed to my bathroom to shower. We were just about to leave when the telephone rang.

"Whoa, hold on, baby girl," I told her as we were stopped in our tracks.

"Daddy, it's getting dark you said. Let's go," she whined.

"Wait a minute, baby," I told her as she began to reach for the doorknob. "C," I greeted.

A shaky hello came through the receiver. It sounded liked Shorty. She was still crying.

"Shorty, what's going on? Are you okay?" I asked, concerned.

"Nothing and no … I mean, I don't know and yes. I am. I don't know. C! My father … my father," she cried. "He's been in a car accident. He's in critical condition! C, Daphne is dead!" She began to cry uncontrollably into the receiver.

The words hit me like ice water. I knew how much Shorty loved her pops. I knew the bond they shared. I knew she was afraid to lose her father. He was the only family she had left. She continued to sob deeply into the phone.

"Daddy," Cupcake sang in the background.

I could feel Shorty's pain. I knew then she needed me without having to ask. "Where are you, Shorty?"

"I'm at the hospital," she whimpered.

"Okay, we're on our way," I told her.

I hated that I had to break Cupcake's heart to tell her we were cancelling our plans. She was so upset and spoiled she began to cry. I hated when she cried. It always made me feel so bad, and she knew that. Her cries became louder, and my thoughts grew heavier. I wondered why Shorty would call me and not her boyfriend. I didn't care, but it was peculiar. I wanted to be there for Shorty. I wanted to keep my promise to my baby girl. Cupcake continued to whine as we got into the car.

I decided to call my sister Vicki. I called her on the way to the hospital. After only a few rings someone answered. "Hello?"

"Hey! Who is this? Where your momma" I asked into the receiver. It was one of my nephews or niece.

"Hey, Uncle C! This Boo. She's in the kitchen. Where Cupcake?" my niece, Boo, stated.

"Hey, princess, she's right here. Put your mom on the phone so she can come over and play."

"Yay, okay! Hold on," she stated and ran off.

"Your auntie is going to pick you up. Okay, baby?" I told her while I waited on my sister to answer.

She smiled and unfolded her arms. I was hoping this could make up for our raincheck.

"Hello," she spoke into the phone.

"Sis, hey. How was your day?"

"It was productive, C. What do you want?" she spit back.

"See, I was trying to be super nice but whatever," I chuckled.

"You're always super nice. But you always want something too," she replied with a laugh.

"I need you to meet me at the hospital to get Cupcake. Emergency with Shorty and her pops," I replied.

"Oh my gosh. Are they okay?"

"I'll tell you more when I see you." Luckily for me, my sister was always my lifesaver.

"Okay, I'm on my way."

Our conversation was then ended. We arrived at the hospital shortly after.

"What's wrong with Pawpaw?" Cupcake asked as we entered the room.

I walked over to Shorty and softly touched her shoulder. "He's hurt, baby," I told her.

Shorty was asleep right next to her father's bed. She was sitting up in the chair, hand in hand with him. She had fallen asleep with a look of worry on her face. Just to think, she looked so vibrant when I'd just seen her. About fifteen minutes later, Vicki stopped by to pick up Cupcake. I filled her in on the heartbreaking news before she whisked Cupcake away.

Shorty remained asleep. I didn't want to wake her, so I took a seat on the couch across from her. She shifted in the chair, and I could tell she was uncomfortable. I wanted to wake her to let her know I was there for her, but she looked restless. I watched her sleep. She was so beautiful. While I stared in her face, she began to open her eyes.

I could see the delight when she realized I was there. She smiled at me. I got up to walk over to her. I held out my arms, and she stood to fill them up. I hugged her tight. She felt so fragile as she began to cry.

"It's okay. Everything is going to be okay," I told her. "You know your pops is a soldier," I whispered as I held her tighter.

"What if he isn't? What if he dies, C? I can't lose him! I just can't," she cried.

"I know, I know," I reassured her.

"I can't lose him, C! I lost my mom! I lost you! I won't have anyone," she yelled.

"You'll have Cupcake. And me. We'll always be here for you," I comforted her.

She continued to sob into my chest. "I don't have you, C. We're not together anymore."

"It doesn't matter if we're together or not. I'll always be there for you, Shorty. I still love you." The words slipped out of my mouth before I could stop them. I didn't plan to speak those words. I was caught by surprise as well and remained silent.

I was ready for her to pull away from me for admitting that. She didn't. She looked up at me. Tears rolling down her face, she asked, "You what, C?"

I hesitated.

She looked at me with curiosity and hope.

I paused and then continued, "I still love you. I never stopped loving you. Believe me, I've tried, but I just can't shake you." The words came and kept coming. "I know you probably thought I hated you, but I don't. I love you too much to ever hate you. I'll never understand why you did what you did. And we don't have to talk about all that right now. Just know that I'm here for you, and I love you, Shorty," I openly told her. It was a relief to get that off my chest.

She looked me in my eyes, as if she were searching for something. "I love you, C. You know I never stopped loving you. I know I cannot apologize enough for what I did and for hurting you. I disappointed you, and I failed my family. I'm sorry," she told me with tears in her eyes.

We locked eyes as we soaked up the words that were finally spoken. We both needed to hear those words. I appreciated that we were both able to reflect on the mistake and possibly move forward. In a sense, it was closure for the both of us. Time had passed us, but those words were needed now. That's the thing with words. They are so simple, yet so powerful.

I pulled her to me and began to kiss her. I couldn't help myself. I pressed my lips against her and instantly felt the spark. Her soft, full lips felt perfect against mine. It had been three years since I'd felt her. Her lips. Her body. Her. She parted her lips and slipped her tongue in my mouth. I cupped her round face with my hand and pulled her closer. She wrapped her arms around me. I could feel her get on her tiptoes as we indulged deeper into the kiss. She was so soft, so sweet. I missed her so much.

We pulled away from the kiss, and I could feel myself getting aroused. I wanted her. I wanted to feel her. She looked up at me. I could see the lust in her eyes. She wanted me too. She felt my nature against her as she reached to caress him, softly and slowly.

"I missed you, C," she told me as she looked down to my manhood and then back up to me.

"Same here, Shorty," I stated. I bent down to kiss her passionately. The moment felt as if it lasted forever. Right there in the hospital room, kissing her, holding her in my arms. Her arms slid from my neck as she began to caress my shoulders and then chest. I nibbled at her bottom lip as I squeezed her plump ass.

I whispered against her lips, "I want you."

She kissed me and replied, "Let's go."

CHAPTER 7

When we arrived in his house, we kissed our way nonstop to the bedroom. Each kiss was filled with intensity and each touch with affection. I'd missed him so much. I missed his touch, his scent. I missed the feel of his lips against mine. I was never really a fan of kissing. But once I met C, he made me enjoy the art of kissing. The intimacy from two lips connecting. Our fire felt as strong as it did back then.

We continued to kiss as he picked me up and carried me upstairs to his bedroom. I placed kisses all over his face as he lay me down on the bed. I wanted him to feel how much I missed him. I wanted him to feel I desired him. I caressed his face as I sucked on his neck. I flicked my tongue against his skin and softly sucked. He reciprocated and sucked on my neck as well.

C sat up to take off his shirt. He revealed his perfectly chiseled body. Just looking at him made me so hot and wet. It had been so long since I'd felt the comfort of a man, the hard body of a man against mine. He got between my legs and slowly came down to kiss me. He kissed me gently. I could feel him grinding against me. That made my pussy throb for him. I wanted to feel him. I wanted him inside of me.

He began to slowly undress me. Peeling off my jeans and shirt and then my crop top. He quickly removed my bra and revealed my breast. His huge hands grabbed both. He covered my nipples with his mouth. I loved the way his warm, wet tongue would roll around my nipples—the way he would nibble softly but suck them hard. He took turns showing both breasts equivalent attention. He began to place kisses down my torso and then past my belly button.

C was such a passionate lover. He playfully bit at my belly button ring. I caressed his head as he continued to kiss his way down. He kissed my thighs. He placed kisses all around my pussy before he filled his mouth with it. He sucked and licked my wetness as I grinded against his face. I loved how he moaned as he pleased me. He spread my legs wider as he licked me all the way down. C was slowly pulling me into his rapture. My body moved without my control as he had his way with it. I came at least twice, and he continued to make my body jerk. He then kissed his way back up to my lips. We kissed, and I was determined to lick all my juices off his face. God, did I miss this man.

He stood up and stared at me as he unbuckled his pants. I felt sexy with him looking at me. I could see in his eyes that he really wanted me. He stood before me, naked. C's body was perfect. He was so big and chiseled—the true definition of tall, dark, and handsome. I could see he had been working out more often. His penis was erect and looked like it wanted to burst. My instinct was to kiss it, caress it, and massage it with my tongue and lips. He looked at his dick and then at me. I knew what he wanted.

I got up from the bed and walked over to him. I stood up on my tiptoes to kiss him. I kissed him deeply and sucked on his tongue. I gently caressed his beard as we kissed passionately. I then began to kiss his jaw, neck, chest, and each ab, and then I squatted. I grabbed his girthy dick with my right hand as I used my left hand to gently touch his leg. I kissed his penis softly and slowly as I lightly licked with my tongue. I wanted to please him. I wanted to make him helpless to me. I could feel his body shudder as my mouth did certain moves. He moaned my name as I used both hands and mouth to satisfy him. I stroked him hard, while I licked his head and caressed his balls. I could feel him about to climax, so I abruptly stopped. He stumbled a bit, and I giggled.

"Why you stop?" he asked with both fist full of my hair.

"Because," I told him, pushing him to the bed, "I want to feel you."

I knew he wanted more, but I didn't care. I wanted him. He fell on the bed, and I climbed on top of him. He ran his hands up my thighs and waist as I positioned myself over him. I gripped his dick and sat down slowly. I used my pelvic muscles to grasp his dick as I went up and down. He massaged my breasts as they bounced. I could feel him fill me up with his dick.

He sat up a little, so he could kiss and suck on my breasts. I leaned down a little to make it easier for him. I could feel myself getting closer to a climax as I continued to go up and down on his well-endowed penis. Before I could stop myself, I was climaxing. C sensed the sensation and immediately flipped us over. My body continued to move hysterically as he began to slowly stroke. He had us in the missionary position. He was kissing on my face, neck, and shoulders as he continued to slowly grind. He felt so good. I stroked his back and shoulders as I sucked on his neck.

He then stopped and looked at me. I could feel tears building in my eyes. The moment was so intimate. We were always so connected when we made love. The emotions and feelings all came back once we linked as one again.

"I love you, Shorty," he whispered as he sustained that slow stroke.

"I love you too," I said as I leaned up to kiss him.

We kissed passionately as he made love just the same. I moved my hips and grinded against him as well. We were in perfect rhythm as we kissed and fucked. C sat up and then flipped me over to my stomach. I loved how he would just take control. He moved my hair away from my face as he kissed me from behind and entered me roughly. He then grabbed a hand full of my curly brown hair as he thrusted himself deeper inside me. He pulled my head back to reveal my face.

"I miss my pussy," he told me as I looked back at him.

"I miss you. I love you, C. This is your pussy," I whimpered as he fucked me harder.

He began to kiss me on my shoulder and run his fingers through my hair. C always loved to see me screaming, moaning louder, and pulling on the sheets. He gripped my waist and then began to spank my ass. I thrusted back. I wanted him deep in this pussy. I wanted to feel all of him.

"Damn, girl," he yelled as he gripped my ass tighter and increased his speed.

I leaned back to kiss him, and he obliged. His mouth covered mine as I could feel sweat drip from his body. Moments later, we both climaxed. We both collapsed on the bed, out of breath and satisfied. He pulled me closer to him and kissed my head. We then fell asleep together.

Hours had passed once I finally woke up. I could hear my pager repeatedly go off. I had to gently ease my way out the bed. C was always easily awakened if he rolled over or reached out in bed and could not feel me. I stood over him and watched him sleep. He looked so sexy and peaceful lying on his back. My pager went off again and interrupted my admiration.

Who could possibly be paging me at this time of the morning? I thought as I quickly ran over to grab it. I was hoping it was the hospital with some good news. It was not. It was Ryan. I couldn't believe he stayed up all night to consistently page me. I contemplated calling him. I'd totally forgotten to return his call once I got word on my father. I didn't want to ruin the beautiful thing we had going. I didn't want to destroy what we were possibly trying to build.

I decided to call him and went downstairs to the living room to do so. Luckily, C's house was huge. I knew he wouldn't hear my conversation with Ryan from downstairs.

"Hello," he greeted roughly on the other end.

"Hey, Ryan," I replied.

"Sydney! Where the hell are you?! I've been waiting on that phone call. You lied to me, Sydney! You lied! Where are you?" he questioned loudly.

I couldn't possibly tell him the truth. I didn't want our relationship to begin built on lies, but my hands were tied. "Calm down, Ryan. You have no idea what is going on. I'm at the hospital," I told him.

"Why? What's wrong?"

"My father was in a horrible car accident. I found out when I was picking up my daughter. I'll be here all night."

"So, when are you going home? When will I see you?"

"I don't know … soon. Maybe this afternoon."

"Okay. I'm sorry for overreacting. I just miss you. You get back in town and then disappear. I was worried. I really care about you, Sydney," he told me sincerely.

I smiled hearing those warm words. Ryan was different, and I liked him. "I know. I care about you too, Ryan," I replied.

"Well, I hope your father gets better. Get some rest, Sydney," he told me and then hung up the phone.

I placed the receiver on the base and realized C was standing in the foyer.

"Come on, let's get back in bed," he offered with his hand extended.

I walked over to grab it. He pulled me to him and picked me up. "You so little," he stated with a kiss as we walked back to the bedroom.

"And you so big," I replied as I kissed him.

We fell asleep kissing, and I woke up to his lips against mine. I opened my eyes, and there he was, handsome as ever.

"Good morning, beautiful. Sleep good?" he greeted.

"Good morning to you, and yes," I replied. I sat up in his massive bed in his huge bedroom.

C renovated and redecorated his entire house after our breakup. This was my first time in his bedroom since that dreadful night. Even the color scheme was different. That was the luxury of being CEO of your own construction company. I liked the fireplace and bay windows he'd added. The fireplace made the bedroom seem cozy. His bedroom appeared beautiful in the morning with all the sunshine entering it. He had several long windows throughout the bedroom.

"I love what you've done with the place," I told him as I sat up.

"Thanks."

"What time is it?"

"Um ... 12:30 p.m."

"Damn," I yelled, jumping out the bed.

"Where are you going? What's wrong?" he asked, watching me look for my clothes.

"Nothing. I just need to go."

"Come on, Shorty. You can at least take a shower before you go," he suggested as he got out the bed. He walked over to me and wrapped his arms around me. He began to kiss and nibble on my ear. C knew exactly what he was doing. That was one of my hot spots.

I entertained the thought of taking a shower with him. It sounded very tempting. I obliged, and soon we were in the shower making love.

C had me pinned against his gray, travertine stone shower wall as he prodded inside me. He pulled my hair as the shower water rained down on us. C made me climax more than I could clean my body. I made him burst, and we exited the shower to dry each other off.

He sat on the edge of his bed in his briefs and asked, "You sure you have to run? We can go get breakfast, or maybe I could cook you breakfast?"

"As much as I would love to take you up on that offer, I should bounce," I told him.

He slipped on some pajama pants and proceeded to walk me to my car. We stood in silence when we reached my gold 1996 Toyota Avalon.

"So, I guess I'll call you later," I told him, as I unlocked my car door.

"Okay," he stated, as he kissed me on the cheek.

By the time I made it home, Ryan had paged me three more times. As soon as I walked through the door, I called the hospital to check on my father. His vitals were stable, but he was still unconscious. I hung up and called over to Vicki's to talk with my Cupcake. She was excited because they were going to the zoo. I promised to get her later, and we would make dinner and bake cookies together. Immediately after I hung up with Cupcake, my telephone rang.

"Oh, so you're home. I've been calling and coming over, and you haven't been there," Ryan yelled into the receiver.

"Ryan, I can explain," I began but was cut off.

"Stay there, Sydney. I'm on my way," he ordered and then hung up.

Thankfully, I had put in for vacation this week after the murder fiasco. I decided to fix myself a bowl of frosted flakes with sliced bananas as I waited on Ryan. Before I could pour my milk, Ryan was banging on the door. The knocks got louder as I walked closer to the door.

"Hold on," I yelled. I opened the door, and it was a furious Ryan.

He looked beyond pissed off and sexy. He obviously had just rolled out of bed or literally been up all night. He wore only a robe, boxers, and socks. He pulled me in his arms and hugged me tightly. He stood back and examined me as if I were hurt or something.

"Ryan, what are you doing?" I asked, laughing.

He looked me dead in my eyes and asked, "Where were you, Sydney? And please don't lie to me. I can see myself being happy with you. I can see us having so much together. Me and you—always. I don't want to ruin this with deceit and lies."

I did not want to lie to him. I did not want to be the liar and cheater—again.

"Sydney," Ryan interjected.

"After the hospital, I went to my father's house. I ended up falling asleep, and I stayed there for the night," I lied.

Ryan grabbed my shoulders and looked me in my eyes. "Sydney, if I find out that you are lying … You will regret it." He pulled me to him and kissed me hard. His face pressed against mine, and the heavy breathing turned me on.

I did not have any intentions of sleeping with Ryan, but it happened. He kissed me and pressed me against the entry door. He touched my body and breasts as he kissed on my neck. I held up my arms as he lifted my crop top. He kissed my cleavage as he grabbed my waist. I took his robe off as he removed my breasts from my pink lace bra. I began to run my fingers over his shoulders and back while he sucked both breasts.

Ryan touched and kissed my body with so much passion and yet aggression. I could feel his desire through his hostility. Ryan bent me over the arm of my sofa and kissed every inch of me as he slid down my jeans. I wanted him. Ryan spanked my ass and forced himself into me. He could not contain himself once he was inside of me. He gripped my ass tighter and sped up his pace. I matched his tempo and forced myself back on him.

"Sydney! Yes, Sydney," he moaned as his body began to shake.

His rhythm was so fast-paced as he banged me roughly. I knew he had peaked as his breathing began to slow. I stood up and turned to kiss him.

"Wow. Sydney, oh my God! You felt so good," he began to tell me.

"No, baby, that was you," I told him with a kiss, "Hey, I need to bathe and run a few errands. I'll call you later."

Luckily, it all worked. Ryan left with a smile, and I left shortly after. I went to sit with my father. I read the newspaper and sang to him. After hours of sitting with him, I left to get my baby girl. I picked her up, and she was more than excited to tell me about her adventure at the zoo. We stopped by the store to get groceries for dinner and headed home.

CHAPTER 8

'Shit,' I thought. I couldn't believe how anxious and nervous I was about a simple date. I was packing up to leave my office as I finalized plans for later. It was a long day, but my excitement for the night made it go by rather quickly. Eventually, I made my way into the infamous Evelyn's schedule. I adored that about her. She was a natural-born hustler. She was about her business and determined to get her practice up and running.

Dr. Evelyn Caro was a dermatologist. She had just recently opened her own practice and was busy getting her brand and name out there. Only a couple of weeks had passed since we'd met. Our conflicting schedules had only allowed us to talk a few times, briefly.

I had a beautiful arrangement made for Evelyn. I also had to stop by the dry cleaners. My goal was to impress her. She initially thought I was a womanizing drug dealer. Yeah, she straight up evaluated me when I asked her out. Little did she know, I was the complete opposite. I had every intention of showing her the difference that night.

"Okay, everyone. Enjoy your weekend. See you guys on Monday," I announced to my staff as I slipped out of the building. I walked through the garage and quickly got into my red Corvette. I left my office to head to the florist. I dropped my top and blasted dope beats through my speakers. My first stop was picking up the flowers, and then I ran to the cleaners to pick up my shirt. Luckily, they were both located in a busy and upscale shopping center on my way home.

I picked up my last minutes and finally headed to the crib. Once home, I poured me a nice glass of cognac over ice and turned on some old school R&B. The music echoed throughout the surround sound in my entire house. I took a long sip from my glass and hopped in the shower.

I exited the shower and stepped into my massive suit closet. I decided to wear one of my favorite custom Italian suits. It was a navy three-piece set. I accompanied it with a bold stripped dress shirt and lavender silk paisley print tie. I finished off my drink as I laced up my oxfords.

Just then, my intercom went off to alert me that my driver for the night had arrived. I picked a vintage, brushed-silver Rolex to wear for the night as I checked the time to see it was only 5:07 p.m. It was a beautiful evening in May, so the weather was perfect. I made my way down the back staircase by way of the kitchen for the arrangement. I decided to leave my cell phone on the credenza in the foyer as I exited my house. I did not want any interruptions, as I planned on entertaining Evelyn for the entire evening.

The driver exited the dark tinted Lincoln Town Car and proceeded to open the back door for me to enter. I gave the driver the directions to her condo downtown. Surprisingly, my excitement diminished as we grew closer to the destination. We pulled up to her building, and I got out to ring her intercom.

"Yes," she spoke into the mike.

"Your knight in shining armor has arrived," I replied with a smile.

"Oh really? Give me like two minutes," she responded with a laugh.

I stood on the sidewalk and observed the scene as I waited. Trail and I owned property a couple blocks from her building. *Funny, that we've never run into each other*, I thought. My thoughts were soon interrupted when Evelyn exited the building. "Wow," was all I could fathom.

She looked stunning each step she took coming down the stairs. She wore her hair straight but pulled to one side. The black knee-length dress hugged her body perfectly. I knew from the fit of the dress it was by one of my favorite designers. It was not tight, but her curves were not hidden. Her black choker only accentuated her long neck and sexy shoulders. Her makeup, if any at all, was flawless.

I reached for her hand as she reached the last step. I spun her around only to reveal her entire back was out. No bra. "You look amazing," I told her as I walked her to the car.

"Why thank you, C. You as well," she told me as she slid in the back seat. I walked around to enter the vehicle and give her the chocolate and flowers I'd brought.

"Thank you! These flowers are beautiful! Oh my gosh," she exclaimed as she looked over the arrangement.

"You're welcome. I'm glad you like them. I hope you enjoy the chocolate as well."

"You have no idea. I absolutely love chocolate! I'm probably going to eat the entire box and cry about it in a corner later," she admitted with a small laugh.

I smiled at her honesty.

"So, I can only imagine what tricks you've got up your sleeves," she stated as she turned toward me and made herself comfortable.

"I have a little something planned. For me, it's been a while since I've been on a real date, so I thought I'd share with you a few things I appreciate in life."

"Oh really? And I'm the lucky lady you decided to take on a real date, huh? I'm curious … Why me?"

I scoffed at her investigation. "A man only dates a woman for one or two reasons. To get to know her or to fuck her," I answered.

"Hm … and which one do I fall under?" she asked.

I smiled. "Neither one. With you, I want both. I want to know everything about you—your dreams, fears, silly antics, favorite food … everything. And then hopefully one day … I can hold you in my arms as I place kisses all over your body and make sweet, passionate love to you. Or rip off your clothes and fuck the shit out of you."

She looked at me with desire and optimism in her eyes. She placed her hand on her chest as she replied. "Well, okay then."

"I hope my bluntness doesn't offend you," I responded.

She softly smiled and spoke. "Of course not. I'm a big girl. I can appreciate a man who can be open and real with his intentions."

We pulled up to the dock shortly after. The driver opened the door for us to exit.

"You didn't tell me we were going for a swim," she stated as she got out.

"We're not," I told her as I took her hand and led her to our yacht. I thought it would be romantic to rent a yacht for a lovely dinner at sunset. I even had a small string band. I mean, that was nothing major. That was just the first half of our date. Of course, I was trying to impress her and show her I was the opposite of what she judged me to be.

We stepped onto the yacht designated for us, and immediately, the band started with soft, classical music. Evelyn looked around amazed by the oversized boat. The captain came over to introduce himself and the crew and/ then quickly ran off. We set sail immediately, as he did not want us to miss the sunset.

"Come on, let's go up top," I told her as I led the way.

The setup was stylish and well-designed. The waiter came to bring us champagne as we stood against the rail.

"Wow, just wow," she stated as she sipped her champagne.

"Do you like it? I really want you to enjoy yourself tonight."

She sipped from her glass once more before she set it on the nearest table. Every move she made had me wanting her more. She was just graceful and sexy all in one. She walked closer to me and stepped up on her tiptoes to kiss me on the cheek. She smelled so delectable.

"This is beautiful, C. Thank you," she told me as she looked me in my eyes.

The waiter then returned with several options of hors d'oeuvres, including bruschetta, carpaccio, and stuffed and fried mushrooms. We took a couple bites from the plate and then took a seat on the luxurious furniture.

"Please sit, relax. Tell me about your day, more about you," I told her as I took a seat next to her.

She smiled and began to open up. With her beautiful exterior, I would've never imagined her to be so deep and down to earth. She told me stories and memories that she had growing up in Cuba. She came to America with her parents and siblings in her teenage years. She was the eldest of four sisters. Evelyn had just finished her last year of vocational training and spent the last nine months starting her own practice. She was also a few years older than me, which I had no issue with. I could date an older woman, especially someone of her quality—someone who understands the strive for building an empire. From listening to her speak so eloquently, I learned she was possessed with tenacity and very passionate about her work.

"Enough about me. I want to know more about you," she stated with a smile and a soft touch.

"What would you like to know?" I asked.

"What do you like to do? It's hard to believe you really listen to classical music ... or is this just a front for the date?" she inquired as she nodded her head to the small group of musicians.

"Come here," I told her as I stood up. I reached for her hand.

She took an appetizer off the serving dish and stood up to join me. The sun had finally begun to set. I led her to the back of the yacht. It was a beautiful setting. The sky reflected several colors from the sun—red, yellow, and orange. The sight was breathtaking. The water only made the moment more picturesque.

"This. This is what I like. Sunsets, sunrises, spending time with my daughter, listening to music, reading and learning, owning shit, you know ... simple things. Moments you capture that turn into beautiful memories," I told her honestly.

She leaned against the rail to soak in the view. "And the music ... Is that to awe me?" she examined.

"Not necessarily. When it comes to music, I'm very eclectic. I enjoy all genres," I replied. I walked closer to her as I pulled her into my arms.

She obliged and sunk into them.

I went on. "Classical music is 432hz music, which is universal harmony. Classical music is known to relax and even help develop the human brain."

"Well, you are not at all what I imagined," she admitted as she looked up to me.

I looked down to her and could feel her getting closer. I could feel she wanted me to kiss her, so I did. I placed my hands on her hips and indulged into her. She bit my lip as she slithered her tongue into my mouth. I gripped her tighter and pulled her closer as I kissed her deeper. I wanted her, but I didn't want to ruin things. I pulled away from the passionate kiss. The attraction was lingering between us hard.

The server then came to announce that our dinner was ready, and we were turning around to head back to the dock. We went inside to eat our three-course meal. We sat at our candlelit table and ate an exquisite meal accompanied with great conversations. I rose my glass to toast. Evelyn rose her glass as well.

"To us. To our first beautiful night together and hopefully not the last," I spoke as our glasses chimed.

"This certainly will not be our last," she whispered as she sipped.

We finished our dinner, and I ordered our dessert to go. I had another part of our date planned elsewhere. We made it back to the dock, and our driver was awaiting us. We got into the sleek black vehicle and headed to our next destination. We soon arrived at the art museum, where a new artist was debuting a collection.

"Oh my gosh, C! I heard about this collection and couldn't get an invite," she oozed as we walked up the stairs.

The curator, a great friend of mine, met us at the door. "Mr. Stone, please come in. We are so glad that you could make it this evening. I hope you have a few minutes later to speak with the artist. I'm sure there are some pieces you will absolutely fall in love with," she told me as she directed us into the museum.

"Thank you, Nadia," I replied.

"Please drink, enjoy, and feel free to ask me for anything you might need," she told us in her thick French accent.

Evelyn immediately walked through the museum to a piece that seemed to call out to her. She looked up at the huge painting in awe.

I quietly walked up behind her and wrapped my arms around her. "What do you see when you look at it?" I whispered.

She was silent for a while, and then she replied, "Well, I absolutely love the colors. So … bright, wild. I see a beautiful woman hiding behind her outer beauty, if that makes sense."

She laughed a little, and I pulled her closer a little. We talked and walked past a few paintings, sharing our perceptions and visions. The night and time slipped away from us quickly.

"C, it's almost midnight," she revealed as if she were Cinderella.

"Will I turn into a pumpkin or something?" I joked.

"No, it's just late, and I have an early morning," she told me.

Time passes quickly when you are truly enjoying yourself. It had been awhile since someone had caught my attention enough to make me feel like time had stopped or didn't exist. I enjoyed the evening with Evelyn. She was different, and I liked every different thing about her.

"I can take you home now if you like," I told her as we walked to the entrance of the museum.

"Yes, that's fine," she stated as she stopped in her tracks. Ironically, we stopped directly in front of the initial painting that had caught her eye. "I really hate I have to end the night so suddenly, but I have an early appointment scheduled in the morning, and—"

"No, I understand. I'm just thankful you allowed me some of your time. I know how busy you are, and I respect the grind," I told her as I held her hands.

"Okay," she sighed.

We exited the building, entered the car, and were at her doorstep in no time. She turned to tell me goodbye as she kissed me softly on my lips.

"Thank you. Tonight, was nothing short of perfect. I feel like I should apologize for judging you originally. You are nothing like what I expected," she stated with a laugh.

"No, I thank you for accepting my invitation. No need to apologize. I took no offense. Truthfully, I took it as a challenge to prove you wrong," I responded with a grin.

She playfully pushed me, and I grabbed her to bring her closer to me. "I hope I don't have to wait weeks on end to see you again," I told her as I wrapped my arms around her waist.

She wrapped her arms around my neck and replied, "No … I will find time for you, Mr. Stone."

I kissed her again, and I could feel my arousal increasing. She pressed her lips softly against mine and slowly licked my bottom lip. She caressed my face with her hands as she kissed me deeper, pressing her body against mine. I could feel her breasts against my chest. I gripped her waist tighter as her hands slid down to rub my chest.

She began to pull away. "I should get to bed."

"Call me tomorrow. Good night, beautiful," I replied as I kissed her forehead. I watched her walk into her building with flowers and chocolate in hand and then disappear into an elevator.

I looked at my Rolex before I got back into the car. It was only fifteen minutes after one o'clock. I wasn't necessarily sleepy, but I was most definitely horny. I wanted Evelyn so bad. She turned me on in ways I thought weren't possible. I was erect almost the entire night just watching her smile, watching her move. She was unknowingly taunting me and making me crave her. Yes, I wanted to strip off her clothes and make passionate love to her. However, she also made me consider a relationship ... again.

Of course, I didn't want to act on my lustful thoughts. I wanted more than a steamy night with her. Admittedly, I didn't know what I wanted from her, which made me want her more. My thoughts did not decrease my erection. I instructed my driver to stop by the nearest pay phone. I needed to dial up my late-night booty call, Keisha.

I met Keisha at a nightclub a few months back. She was a cool, hood, thick chick who answered every time I called—no matter what time. We pulled over to a service station that had a couple of pay phones on the side of the building. I reached in my pocket to search for a quarter. Luckily, I had one and stepped out of the car to make the call. I dialed up her digits, and she picked up after a couple of rings.

"Hello," she greeted.

"Keisha, wut's up? This C."

"Oh, hey, C! Wut's up with yo' sexy ass?"

"You. Mind if I slide through?"

"Of course, I don't mind. I'll leave the door unlocked, I'm 'bout to slip into the shower," she told me and then hung up.

I gave my driver directions as I got into the car. Keisha was my go-to. I went to her if didn't feel like entertaining a new chick but wanted the company or pleasure of a woman. She never asked for anything. That's why I would always throw her something if I came through. We pulled into the apartment complex where she stayed. It was late at night, but some people were still hanging out.

I instructed my driver to come back after I paged him. I left my jacket in the car and walked up to Keisha's door. Just as promised, it was unlocked. I could smell the scent of hydro weed as I walked into her small one-bedroom apartment. She had most of the lights out, and only the television in the living room was on. I could hear water from the shower as I walked to her bedroom.

"C, is that you?" she yelled from behind the shower curtain.

"Yeah," I answered as I entered her room.

"I rolled you up a blunt. It's on the nightstand. Make yourself at home. I'll be out in a minute!"

I began to take off my vest as I loosened my tie. I went to get the blunt from her nightstand. I lit up the tightly rolled, marijuana-filled cigar. I inhaled the smoke as I took a seat and exhaled the smoke as I laid back onto her bed. My body seemed to cover her entire queen-sized frame. I took a few more puffs before I could hear the shower water turn off.

She stepped into her bedroom wearing nothing but drips of water. She walked over to me and proceeded to take off my shoes. She then unbuckled my belt and undid my pants. I continued to smoke my blunt as she unbuttoned my shirt and removed my tie. Soon, I was lying across her bed in only my briefs and tank top.

My blunt was half smoked by the time she covered my dick with her mouth. Keisha could suck a dick and get nasty. I liked that about her. Once she felt I was hard enough for her, she reached for the condom to slide it on my dick. She then climbed on top to ride me. I could feel her wet pussy slowly slide down my hard shaft. She began to bounce up and down as she began to moan and scream. I gripped her ass tighter as I assisted her to bounce on my dick. I could feel her body trembling as she was releasing her climax.

I flipped over so I could be on top of her. I sat up and pushed her legs back as I began to drill that pussy. I fucked her for a few more positions, and in some instances, I imagined her as Evelyn. The more intense my thoughts became, the more intimate I became with her. I kissed her shoulders and caressed her hair as I started to stroke her slowly. Immediately after, I burst.

"Damn, C," she sighed as she collapsed against the bed.

I hopped up to wash up. I paged my driver before I started to get dressed. Keisha was drifting off, as usual. I left a few hundred on her nightstand, kissed her cheek, and left out the back door. I walked through my front door shortly after. I didn't even attempt to climb the stairs to my bedroom. I walked to the nearest guestroom downstairs and passed out.

CHAPTER 9

I couldn't believe I was standing at the burial of my father's long-time girlfriend, Daphne. Without my father, nonetheless. It had been a week and a few days since the fatal accident. My father was still unresponsive and in a coma. I stood over the casket quietly as they slowly lowered it into the ground. I wiped the tears from my eyes with my left hand, as Ryan tightly held my right. I whimpered as I threw my rose in the grave and walked away from the hole in the ground, now filled with the woman my father once loved.

I hated the fact that my father had to wake up to the news that his darling Daphne was now dead. Although they never married within their three-year relationship, I knew my father loved her. He never remarried after my mother. My father had been through so much in life. And now to lose another love … I could only imagine his pain.

Ryan pulled me closer to him as we walked across the wet grass to his car. He hugged me tightly and kissed my cheek before he assisted me into the passenger seat of his 1996 Lincoln Continental.

"It's going to be okay, Sydney. I'm here for you," Ryan soothed, as he got into the car. He grabbed my hand and kissed it. "I know you didn't want to attend the repast, so I have an entire day planned for us," he assured me as we pulled off the cemetery lot.

I was quiet most of the ride, just trying to process my thoughts. Life was changing. I didn't know if I was accepting or afraid of the change. I looked at all the buildings passing as we drove by. I didn't know how I was feeling. I had so much on my mind lately. My father, running the company in his absence, C, Ryan … just everything. Ryan and I seemed as if we were becoming serious, yet my mind still wandered back to the passionate night C and I shared.

"Babe, I'm going to pick up Cori so we can have a family day," I barely heard Ryan announce.

I was still recollecting the conversation that C and I shared, especially the fact that he told me he still loved me. I didn't know whether to believe him. I knew my love for him was still real, so I could only hope his love survived as well. The way he touched me and made love to my body suggested that we were still very much in love. I could feel myself toying with the thought of C and I being a couple once again, even though it felt like Ryan and I were practically already a couple. C and I had history, yet Ryan and I had chemistry. My heart felt like it was being torn between two men. It was becoming hard to see my future when it came to my love life.

We pulled up at a Shay's boutique before I realized we were in the neighborhood. I saw Shay and Cupcake through the long glass windows. They were hanging clothes on a mannequin. Ryan came around to open the door for me. As we entered the store, I saw pure delight in my daughter's face. Her eyes were bright, and she had a huge smile. She enjoyed dressing the mannequins as if they were her full-sized dolls.

"Momma," she yelled as she ran to me.

I squatted to scoop her up into my arms. I held her so tightly.

"I missed you, Momma. Love you," she told me. She then placed kisses all over my face.

"I love you more, baby—my sweet little Cupcake," I replied with a kiss on her cheek.

"Hey, Cori," Ryan said from behind me.

"Hey, Ryan! My name is Cupcake," she told him.

"Come, Momma! Look at what I did," she begged as she dragged me to her personal model. I happily followed.

"Hey girl," Shay greeted with a small hug. "How are you holding up?" she asked.

"I'm okay," I admitted.

She grabbed my hand and gave me a reassuring squeeze. I appreciated that small gesture. I cherished my friend. Shay was always there for me—always the big sister I never had.

"What are you doing here?" she asked.

"Oh, yeah. Here to get Cupcake."

"No, you can't take my baby. I thought I was going to have her all day," Shay stated as she ran to wrap Cupcake in her arms.

She laughed at her godmother.

"I just want to chill and be around my baby right now. Just be around love," I told her. I just wanted to enjoy time with my daughter.

"I understand," she replied as she kissed Cupcake on her head. "Cupcake, go get your bag baby, and then you can help me put your model in the front window," she instructed.

Cupcake ran to the back office with glee. I smiled at my beautiful baby's enthusiasm. Shay crept up beside me as she nodded toward Ryan. "So. … are you guy's official or what?" she asked.

I glanced over to see him looking over pieces and price tags, hopefully creating a wish list for me and my birthday. "I don't know. I mean … I like him. He fine, and he good to me," I declared.

He looked over and smiled at me as if he could hear our private conversation. It was something about our connection. I smiled back at him.

"Okay, TeTe! I'm back. I'm ready," Cupcake yelled as she came running back into the showroom.

"Well, I'm going to say this. If you not that into him, he's really into you, Shorty. You see the way he looks at you? That boy looks sprung," she stated with a small laugh.

I laughed with her. It was funny because Ryan was beginning to behave as if he were sprung. It wasn't a terrible thing. Of course, I wanted a man head over heels in love with me. What woman wouldn't? However, things were moving so fast. Ryan's feelings for me were growing so rapidly. He was adamant that we were meant to be together.

I often thought about my failed relationship with C. I wondered if this could be my rebound at love again. Could this be my happy ending? I was always compelled to think that I would never find true love again. Believing that because of my infidelity, a man would never love me. I fucked over a good man and punished myself with the idea that I would never find another good man and that a man would never love and appreciate me again.

I looked over to Ryan and smiled. Shay and Cupcake began to move the mannequin dressed in leopard print and pink to the front display. Cupcake was excited to run outside and look at her model from the sidewalk. I picked up her belongings, and Ryan followed me outside.

"Momma, look! I did that," she exclaimed. She jumped up and down and giggled.

"I see, boo. I love it," I told her.

Shay kissed and hugged my baby some more. "Shorty, call me later. We should do lunch tomorrow."

"Okay, girl, I will. Thanks again! Love ya," I told her as we drove off.

Ryan had the entire evening planned for us, to my surprise. I was appreciative that Ryan was willing to accept my daughter and I as a package deal. He told me he wanted to cheer me up and spend more time with Cupcake. Not only did he have a fun-filled day planned, but he even had matching outfits for us all to wear. We stopped by his condo to change into identical blue jeans, multicolored striped tops, and white Reeboks.

The motion caught me off guard. It was odd that he already knew our sizes, but I was grateful I had something to change into. I didn't want to walk around looking like I just left a funeral. We looked like we were on our way for family portraits instead of mini golf. Luckily, he didn't have our faces air brushed on anything.

We entered the huge, colorful golf course, and Cupcake took off running with her bright pink golf club in hand. She ran to the first stop on the mini golf journey. "My turn first," Cupcake shouted.

"I'm next," Ryan playfully announced.

"Well, I guess I'll have to go last, huh?" I replied with a smile.

I enjoyed watching Ryan play and have fun with Cupcake. I was very skeptical initially about allowing Ryan to meet her. She had never seen any man around me outside of her father. I knew this was going to be new for her, just as it was for me. I had to get back into the idea of dating. I couldn't waste my entire life waiting for C.

It had been almost a month since we'd started dating, and I really liked Ryan. Undeniably, Cupcake was a bit standoffish when she met him, but she is goofy and playful. Once she realized Ryan was practically a giant playdate, she was more accepting of him. Cupcake found joy in anything and anybody. She was always such a happy child. I adored the innocence of her youth. I could remember being a child and having no worries—none whatsoever. Just going to school, cleaning my room, and being happy. I wish life were that simple again. The older you get, the more complicated life appears. Although, life is what you make it.

As a child, the word *love* was just that. The word, *love*. I mean, I knew what is was to love my father. I can recollect almost no memories of my mother; however, I knew I felt some type of love for her as well. I had to fall in love, love, and be loved and then have a child to truly understand an influential energy like love. Love is one of the most powerful forces in the universe. I found myself in deep thought a lot lately. I didn't know if it was the funeral, my father's critical condition, or my torn love life that made my mind wander into yonder.

Then a disgusting, nauseous feeling hit me. I needed to take a seat. "Babe, you guys enjoy the next few rounds. Let me sit down for a minute," I told them as I went to sit at the nearest bench.

Before I could sit and get comfortable on the oddly shaped bench, I could hear someone yell my name. "Yo, Shorty!"

I looked over to see it was Trail and a group of teenage boys. I'm sure the group of young gentlemen were from his community center. Now that is one thing I will forever commend Trail on. Trail was an OG, hood nigga, but he was a hood nigga who gave back and essentially bought back the hood. Trail progressed from the dope game to the corporate game and became the most respected guy in the city doing such. Trail was the mastermind behind C. He saw the potential and talent in C as a young street nigga, and he molded him into the man he was today.

"Good evening, ma'am." The boys spoke almost simultaneously.

"Good evening, fellas." I then stood up to hug Trail.

"Y'all go and play some games. I'll catch up," Trail instructed.

He reached into his Iceberg jeans to pull out a wad of cash. He peeled it back and handed the boys a few bills. They immediately ran off, eager to play. I will always have admiration and respect for him.

"Long time, no see," he said to me.

"I know. Seems like forever, huh?"

"It does. Yo, I heard about yo' pops and his old lady. You know if you need anything …"

"Yeah, I know. Thank you, Trail."

Almost seconds later, I could hear Cupcake screaming, "Uncle Trail!" She ran over to him and gave her godfather a big hug.

Ryan came out of nowhere. "Who is this?"

Trail looked at me and then to Ryan. "This my girl Shorty. Who is you?"

"Your girl?" Ryan spit back.

"Trail, this is my friend Ryan. Ryan, this is Trail," I introduced.

There was an awkward pause.

"Well, Shorty, it was good seeing you. CC, I know I'll see you soon, baby girl," Trail stated with a grin as he walked off.

"Momma, I'm hungry," Cupcake told me as she tugged at my hand.

"Okay, come on, baby. Let's get something to eat."

We then walked off to the food court. I could feel Ryan's gaze behind me. I could feel his jealously and curiosity of who the man he'd just met was. He pulled my arm and stopped me in my tracks. Cupcake continued to run to the food court.

"Your friend," he stated as he held my arm.

"Ryan, we're not doing this here," I told him as I pulled my arm from his grasp.

"Sydney, I just feel that it's disrespectful to introduce me as your friend! What kind of bullshit is that?! And you still haven't told me who he is," he stated seriously.

"Ryan, how can I introduce you as anything other than a friend? We have never sat to discuss our status. We're friends," I deplored.

"Well, maybe that's something we need to sit down to discuss. I feel like we are more than friends. You know how I feel about you, Sydney."

"I understand that, Ryan. However, just because you feel a certain way doesn't mean we're supposed to rush into a relationship. Yes, we should have a conversation about where this could go, but I'm happy with where we are now. Maybe. One day. Not here and not now," I told him as I walked off to join my baby at the counter.

I didn't know if he was upset with my response. Quite frankly, I didn't care. I was being real with him. We ordered our food, and by the time we sat to eat, my cellular phone rang.

"Hello," I greeted.

"Hi, is this Sydney Inox? This is Beverly from Fran Chester Hospital. Your father has awakened," she spoke into the phone.

I dropped my phone on the table in disbelief as I began to flow with tears and screams of joy.

"Hello … hello?" I could barely hear from the speaker.

Ryan picked up the phone and spoke to the nurse on my behalf. I was overcome with emotions. My father was alive and awake. I could talk to him. I could hug him. Cupcake continued to stuff her mouth with her corndog and fries as she looked at me.

"Momma, why are you smiling and crying?" she asked so innocently.

I laughed and answered her. "Because Pawpaw is up and ready to see us!"

I wanted to see my father immediately. I needed to see him. I got to-go boxes for our food and had Ryan hurry us to the hospital. We arrived rather quickly, and before Ryan could get out of the car, I grabbed his arm.

"Wait. Why don't you just drop us off, and I'll call you tomorrow," I offered.

"What? What do you mean? What are you talking about, Sydney? Is this about earlier?" he asked, with a confused stare.

"No. Not at all. You know … I just think right now isn't the best time for you to meet my father. He needs rest, and you know I need to talk to him about Daphne. It's just a lot right now, and I don't want to add to it," I explained to him.

I wasn't ready for him to meet my father—not yet. And not under these circumstances. I wasn't ready for my father's approval or disapproval of him.

"I'm sorry for overreacting. I just want to be there for you, Sydney," he told me as he grabbed my hand.

"And you have been. You are. I appreciate you, Ryan. I just need to do this alone. I'll probably be here all night," I declared. I reached over the console to kiss his cheek. "Thank you for everything. I mean that. I'll call you later," I told him, as I exited the car.

"Come on, Cupcake," I stated as I opened the back door for her.

"Bye, Ryan," she stated, hopping out the vehicle.

"See you later, pretty girl," he told her with a wave.

Cupcake and I entered the hospital, and I decided to stop by the gift shop to get him fresh flowers and balloons, and Cupcake picked him out a teddy bear. Gifts in hand, we proceeded to the wing where my father was held. I didn't know where I was going to start with him. So much had changed since he had been out. I opened the door to his room. He was sitting up, and when he saw me, a smile spread across his face.

"Daddy," I yelled as I ran across the room to hug him tightly.

He hugged me back just as tightly. In a split second, everything felt as if it was going to be all right.

CHAPTER 10

Shit, I thought I was busy, but Evelyn had me beat. A week after our date I had to go to Philadelphia to oversee a huge demolition project. It had almost been a month since our date, and I hadn't seen her since. Before I made it back, she had already left for a conference. I enjoyed the few hours she'd take out of her day to talk. I loved the deep, long conversations I had with her. We could talk about anything and everything.

I loved the way her mind worked. She was brilliant and beautiful. The absence of me not seeing her was not only increasing my anticipation but turning me on. I don't get it, so don't judge me. Every time we talked, she expressed how it was the best date in her life. I knew she hated that our schedules were so conflicting, but I assured her it was fine. I was patient and understanding.

It was a beautiful Tuesday afternoon, and I was chilling at the crib. I decided to invite Keisha over for a swim. It was my first time inviting any woman to my home. I'd taken a few chicks to my loft downtown but never here. Keisha and I had been kicking it for months now, and I could use the company and entertainment. I was in my bedroom, slipping on a pair of blue-and-yellow striped Nautica trunks when the telephone rang.

"C," I greeted.

"You just never seem to stop amazing me, huh?" Evelyn spoke from the other end.

I smiled because I knew she must've received her gift. "What do you mean?" I asked.

"Well, I just made it back in town today … and I get home to this huge, magnificent painting. C, this is the painting from our date night—the one I fell in love with," she stated softly.

"I know. I remembered how much you liked it."

"But C … this … This is an overgenerous gift. You didn't have to do that."

"Of course, I did. No money adds up to making someone you like smile," I admitted.

"Oh, C," she gushed.

I could hear her smile through the phone. That made me happy. Then my doorbell rang.

"Look, I know you just got back in town. Go ahead and get settled in, and let me send a car for you tomorrow," I offered. I was hoping she would finally have the time and accept this attempt at a second date.

"Yes, okay. What time should I be ready?" she asked.

"It's up to you. Why don't you unpack, relax, and call me later," I told her.

"Okay. Thank you again, C. I can't wait to see you tomorrow. I'll call you later," she responded and then hung up.

I rushed downstairs as the doorbell rang for a second time. I opened the door, and it was Keisha. There she stood holding her beach bag and wearing her neon-colored bikini and matching wrap skirt. The skirt was fishnet, and I could see every inch she was attempting to hide. She walked past me, taller than usual in her white sandals.

"Sorry to keep you waiting," I greeted as she stepped in.

"You good. It took me a while to find your house. Feel like I kept you waiting," she joked.

"I was hoping you could follow directions," I clowned back.

She playfully pushed me as I closed the front door. "I ordered us some takeout that should be here later, but we can head outside if you not scared," I told her as I grabbed her hand to lead the way.

"Whatever … I ain't never scared," she huffed.

We walked through the kitchen and out the back door to the pool.

"Wow, C! Your house is so big and nice! I love this pool," she exclaimed as we entered my backyard oasis.

My courtyard was incredible. My home sat on five beautiful

acres. My mountain-style pool was accompanied with a natural stone grotto and spectacular waterfall. The lush landscaping captured the quintessential natural style I was aiming for. Growing up in the ghetto with nothing made me strive to only want the best. I worked hard for it, and I deserved it.

"Thanks," I replied before I dove into the water. I emerged and swam a couple laps across the pool.

Keisha just stood there looking at the water.

"You do know nothing is going to jump out at you, right?" I joked, still floating in the water.

She stepped forward to dip her left foot in. "It's cold," she shuddered.

"It's not that cold. You got to get in and get comfortable with the water," I informed her. I then swam over to the bank near her. "Come on, it's not that cold," I replied, throwing water on her legs.

"C! Stop," she ordered as she stepped back with a smile.

"Come on, please get in," I begged, pulling at her legs.

"No, it's too cold. I can just sit out here and look cute," she responded, stepping back.

I then took off my trunks and threw them at her feet.

"That's supposed to make me get in?" she quizzed, looking down at my only piece of clothing.

"Yeah," I spit back.

She slowly took off her heels and cover-up and then got into the pool.

"If you go under, it won't seem so cold," I advised.

Keisha had her hair cut into a sexy short style. "What about my hair?" she asked, attempting to pat her do.

"What about it? I'll take care of that. You know I got you," I declared.

She finally went under the water. Seconds later, she came back up.

"See, now that wasn't so hard, was it?" I asked.

She shook her head with a smile. "Although, I do feel overdressed," she stated as she started to take off her brightly colored top. She then took off her bikini bottoms.

"It's going to be hard teaching you how to swim with all that distraction," I replied.

"It's cool. If it gets hard, I can make it soft again," she told me seductively.

A few laps around the pool, and before long, we were in the jacuzzi. We were both naked and horny, and the jacuzzi only made the moment more erogenous.

"Wait, C. Let me get the bottle and the rubbers," she announced as she hopped up to get the items.

She sipped from the cognac bottle and passed it to me before she hopped back in. I sipped from the bottle as she opened and put on the condom. I bent Keisha over in the hot tub and thrust myself into her. Before I could climax, Keisha jumped off my dick.

"Whoa," I breathed.

She then sat me down and hopped on me to ride this dick. I was enjoying fucking Keisha. She became my regular slide, even though my mind would revert to Shorty sometimes. My thoughts drifted away as her moans became louder. She reached her point, climaxed, and collapsed. I held her in my arms as I continued to slowly stroke. The doorbell rang through the speakers before I could burst.

"I bet it's the food," she whispered.

"Shit, I almost forgot," I replied as I kissed her shoulders. I gripped her ass and glided her up and down. I could feel her body shiver as I placed kisses on her breast.

The doorbell rang again.

"I'll get it," Keisha offered as she began to get up.

I had robes, fruit, liquor, the whole spread laid out for us. Keisha slid into the white, terry cloth robe and tightened the belt. She ran her fingers through her short hair and blew me a kiss before she walked off.

I laid back, delighted in the moment. I was at a wonderful place in life. My daughter was healthy and happy. My business was growing and thriving. My charity was a phenomenal success. I could volunteer more in the community. I was even happy with the current status of my single life. I stood up to get out the jacuzzi and put on my robe. I could hear faint yelling. I shook my head as I walked toward the house, thinking Keisha was arguing with the delivery guy. I knew Keisha was a bit hood, and I liked that about her. As I entered the house and walked through the kitchen, the yelling was loud and obvious. It was Shorty and Keisha. I saw that Shorty had Cupcake with her too as I entered the foyer.

"Hold up, hold up," I interjected. "What's all this hollering for?!" I looked down to my baby girl and saw that she was scared. I picked her up, and she laid her head on my shoulders. "Shorty, why the fuck you over here acting like this, scaring my baby and shit?" I asked as Cupcake tightened her arms around my neck.

"We're leaving anyway. Give me my baby," she demanded as she attempted to take her from my arms.

She was furious. I could see it in her face. "No. What's going on? Why are you popping up over here anyway?" I inquired.

"It doesn't matter. We're interrupting, so we're leaving," she replied as she snatched Cupcake.

Keisha rolled her eyes and walked off. Shorty stormed out of the door and to the car with our daughter in her arms.

I followed her. "Shorty! Shorty! Why are you mad?" I quizzed as she buckled Cupcake into the car seat.

"Who is that, C?" she asked with jealousy in her eyes.

"What? That's Keisha," I answered.

"So, I guess you're in a relationship now. I didn't know about her! You didn't tell me anything," she screamed.

"Wait, hold up, Shorty. You cannot come over to my house, demanding I tell you who I do or do not fuck with. That's none of your damn business," I remarked.

She was rabid. Her face was flustered and red. She then looked past me with anger. Keisha was standing in the doorway.

"He good! He don't need you supervising," Shorty yelled to her.

"Whatever, lil girl. When he's done talking to baby momma, he'll be in here with me. Go cry about it, bitch," Keisha spat back.

"Come treat me like a bitch, bitch," Shorty threatened as she walked toward Keisha.

I jumped in front of her. "Shorty, go home," I told her, pushing her back toward her car.

"Get the fuck off me, C! Now," she screamed.

I couldn't believe she was reacting this way.

"Let her go," Keisha yelled from behind me.

They were both yelling deadly threats as I stood between them. I was finally able to get Shorty into her car. Cupcake was crying, Shorty was mad as hell, and I was mostly confused.

"Shorty, you gonna have to calm down. Why you acting like this in front of our baby? Is everything okay?" I asked.

She finally began to sit still and breathe slowly. She was silent. I then saw a tear roll down her cheek. I tried to wipe the single tear away, but she turned her head from my hand. I then walked to the rear door to console my daughter.

"It's okay, baby," I soothed her. She was crying as I squatted in the car to hug her. I held her in my arms. My prize, my own. She was afraid, and I knew it. "Everything is going to be fine, baby. Okay? Stop crying," I assured, as I wiped her tears.

"Daddy, Momma gonna be okay too?" she asked.

"Yeah, Momma is fine."

"We're leaving," Shorty announced in between tears.

I kissed my baby and closed the door. I then stood at Shorty's open window. She was crying, and I felt guilty.

"I can't believe you, C," she reported with a sigh.

"What are you talking about? I haven't done anything out of line," I reassured her.

"Bullshit," she yelled. "You lied, C! You had me thinking and believing that you really love me."

She was dead serious. I truly didn't understand where she was coming from. She was practically in a relationship with another man. "I do, Shorty. You can't question that I love you. You know how I feel, what I've shown you, proven to you. Facts never change," I told her frankly.

She flared her nose and rolled her beautiful brown eyes. I was distracted by the natural, yet sexy I'm-mad-as-hell gesture.

"Whatever, C! Let's not forget you also lied about being single! Why lie about that just to fuck?"

I couldn't believe Shorty. She was acting delusional and very defensive. "Shorty, you know that's not how I get down. We need to talk another time if you feel unsure about some shit."

"Go on back in there with your lil hood rat," she directed.

Then the delivery driver pulled into the driveway. Shorty saw the mobile food drop-off from her rearview mirror. "Let me go. We're clearly interrupting," she replied as she cranked the car and peeled off.

I got the food from the delivery driver and went into the house. I sat the three-course Chinese meal on the kitchen island. Keisha was walking around the kitchen, still speaking ill of Shorty. I did not want to hear that shit. I called her over to set up the dinner table. She unpackaged all the food and put it into the serving dishes. She had the table laid out. I picked over the egg rolls. I barely had an appetite anymore. She stuffed her mouth and continued to talk shit, so I went into the living room.

I rolled up a blunt to ease my mind. I could hear her in the kitchen cleaning dishes and putting away leftovers. I inhaled the smoke, and my thoughts drifted to the crazy scene with Shorty. I exhaled and wondered why she would react in such a way. My confusion decreased as my altitude increased.

Keisha then entered the room. She had two glasses in her hands. "Here," she stated as she handed me the cocktail.

"Thanks," I replied as I passed her the blunt.

She laid across the couch on me. It seemed that she had finally calmed down. The room was quiet and smoked out.

"Do you and yo' baby momma still talk?" she asked, passing the blunt.

"As parents, yeah."

"Oh," she sighed.

Here come the questions, I thought.

"I just find it mighty strange," she started as she began to sit up, "that she was acting like that, and y'all don't even talk. Do you still love her?"

Now this was a trick question. I could lie to her and myself and say no. Or I could be honest and tell her yes. Although, I know there would be so much more to follow that. I thought long and hard and answered her, "Look, Keisha, don't do that. You didn't make the situation no better. That's my daughter's mother. Of course I got love for her, but not like that. And I don't appreciate all these damn questions."

"You right, C. You right. My bad, let me make it up to you," she proclaimed. She then began to undue my robe. I laid back on the couch. Before I knew it, her head was in my lap. She sucked my dick with such devotion. She made sure I felt her apology. I came, and she swallowed. I was tired and high. She was still sitting up watching TV.

I was awakened from the sound of Keisha yelling. I looked over and saw she was on the telephone.

"I don't give a fuck! Bring yo' ass on," she screamed into the receiver.

Keisha had changed into a white T-shirt with a sunflower print sundress over it. I sat up on the couch, dazed and confused.

"Yeah, whatever! Whatever," I heard her repeating.

"Keisha, who is that?"

She turned and looked at me. She had that sexy, mad look. "Some bitch," she answered, more into the receiver, though.

I snatched my telephone away from her and greeted, "Who is this?"

"Put that bitch back on the phone," a familiar voice told me.

"Who is this?" I asked again.

"Who the fuck you think?" the person yelled.

I then recognized the voice as Jaz's. *Shit. Shorty got this unstable-ass creature involved.*

"Put that hoe back on the phone, C," she ordered.

"Where is Shorty?"

"It doesn't matter. She not with yo' dog ass!"

"Put her on the phone, Jaz!"

"She doesn't want to talk to yo' ass!"

"Look, put her on the phone now," I demanded.

Keisha was in the background talking mad shit about Shorty.

"What?" Shorty roared in my ear.

"What's up, Shorty? What's all this shit about?" I asked.

"Shit, you tell me," she proclaimed with an attitude.

"Why are you calling my house and starting shit?"

"I'm not starting shit! If anything, I'm gonna finish it," she answered.

This was bizarre. Shorty had never behaved like this. It was as if her crazy-ass homegirl had taken over her.

"Where your girlfriend at?" Shorty asked, interrupting my thoughts.

I didn't want to answer her. I didn't want to entertain this bullshit.

"Shorty, we need to talk. You and me. Not Keisha or Jaz. Just us," I advised.

"No! We don't have anything to talk about. You lied to me, C! You hurt me!"

"I didn't lie to you! You need to calm down, Shorty."

"Whatever," she commented. She was then silent.

I didn't know what else to say but, "You out here dressed all like a family and shit with my daughter and the next nigga but want to trip because I'm doing my own thing? You never told me about him, and I never got mad." I couldn't believe we were having this conversation. I didn't have to explain this to her. I didn't have to explain myself to anyone. This was insane.

"You did get mad, C! You got mad the night you met him," she spit back.

"No, I was never mad. He was trying to be disrespectful, and I handled it accordingly."

"Whatever," she repeated.

"Tell that slut we on our way," Jaz announced from the other end. The conversation was then ended.

Shit, I thought. I looked at Keisha. She was deranged. "Keisha, I think you need to go home," I suggested, getting up.

"Why?! Them hoes on they way?" she quizzed, standing up also.

"Why would you answer my phone anyway? You not helping the situation, entertaining they bullshit," I answered her.

"The telephone kept ringing. I didn't know if it was an emergency or not. I know you have a baby and a business. I thought I was helping," she replied.

I ran upstairs to my bedroom to change. I threw on a pair of tennis shoes, sweatpants, and a tank. When I came back down, I had to convince Keisha to go home. She was adamant that she was not "scared of them hoes." By the time we were leaving out the door, I could see Jaz's red Lincoln Navigator approaching. It came to a complete stop in my driveway.

Shit, I thought. "Keisha, go back in the house," I ordered.

"Hell no! I am not running from them hoes," she said proudly.

Shorty and Jaz then jumped out of the vehicle. Before I knew it, we were all facing one another.

"This that bitch, Shorty?" Jaz quizzed, looking Keisha up and down.

"Yep. That's her."

As soon as Shorty answered the question, Jaz hit Keisha in the mouth. From there, all three were fighting. I had to do my best to keep them apart, as they were trying to jump Keisha. Minutes passed before I could get them separated. Keisha rushed Shorty and sucker punched her. Jaz ran over to jump in, and as I was pulling Keisha away, she kicked Shorty in her stomach.

Falling to the ground, Shorty began to hold her stomach in pain. Jaz immediately ran to her side. Looking up to Keisha, Jaz broadcasted, "You stupid bitch! She's pregnant!"

The words hit me hard. I was stunned by the announcement and lost track of keeping the girls apart. I looked at Shorty as she sat on the pavement, holding her belly. Jaz and Keisha were fighting behind me. I couldn't believe she was pregnant and I didn't know. I couldn't believe she was pregnant by that lame. I walked over to her. I extended my hand, and she took it.

"Why didn't you tell me you were pregnant?" I asked.

She said nothing. I just stared her in the face. Her scars were visible, so I knew she didn't have on any makeup.

"Were you even going to tell me you were pregnant?"

She humped her shoulders.

"You don't have to keep anything away from me like that, Shorty. I'll still be here for you, even though it's not mine," I told her.

She gave me a look. Her look made me remember what we did over a month ago.

"Wait. Is it mine?" I asked her seriously.

She then dropped her head and humped her shoulders.

"Shorty, are you pregnant with my baby?" I asked with my hand on her shoulders.

Before she could answer the question, there was a gunshot. I had completely forgot about Jaz and Keisha fighting. I turned around to see Jaz holding a gun. Glancing Keisha's body over, I was glad she wasn't hit.

"Jaz, let's go," Shorty requested.

"Okay," Jaz agreed.

Shorty and Jaz began to walk to the SUV.

"Ol' stupid-ass bitch! Fighting over a nigga don't even love or want yo' dumb ass," Keisha screamed at them.

The words stopped Shorty in her tracks. Jaz turned to raise her gun. Shorty stopped her and mumbled some words, and they hopped in the truck and drove off.

"Fuck," I roared. "Why the hell you have to go and say all that for?!"

"What you mean?" Keisha spit back.

"Nothing, nothing," I repeated. "Keisha, go home." I watched her roll off and then went inside. Today was fucked up. The day I finally decided to invite a woman to my home, and this shit happened. Shorty was acting like a complete lunatic, and Keisha stooped right down to her level. After a day like this, I was anxious for tomorrow.

CHAPTER 11

How could I allow myself to step out of character like that? I couldn't get the scenario of what happened the night before last, out of my head. I scrubbed harder on the countertop as my thoughts played the entire evening back. I decided to stop by C's house after picking up Cupcake from summer camp. Some random chick answered his door. Her mouth got reckless. And before I knew it, Jaz was there, and we were all fighting and arguing.

My emotions had been all over the place lately. The pregnancy was to blame for all of this, I believed. I found out I was pregnant only days before Jaz announced it in front of C. I didn't want C to know I was pregnant. Hell, I didn't want to be pregnant. And under my circumstances, I really didn't need to be pregnant. I sighed and shook my head as I proceeded to clean the cabinets. My anxiety was through the roof, and cleaning was one of the only activities that relaxed me. Irregular bleeding is what prompted me to go to the doctor last week. It was crazy. I practiced abstinence for three years, and when I do decide to sex again … not only did I screw two men, but now I was pregnant. And, no, I didn't know who the father was. I had unprotected sex with two men and didn't consider the outcome.

My life was becoming so complicated lately. I missed the simplicity of what was once my life. At this point, I knew that was long gone. It was the third house I'd cleaned today. I decided to take a break from the office and get out to clean a few properties. C hadn't called me, and I refused to call him. For some odd reason, I was furious with him,

90

more so than that random woman. I didn't know what or how what happened transpired.

I felt upset that she was over at his house. I knew C wasn't going to call me, and he knew I wasn't going to call him. And here we began the cycle of guilty pride. I ran warm water over my sponge as I begin to drift into my thoughts. This is what we did. This started early in our relationship and now into our coparenting relationship. This cycle could go on for days, even weeks.

Something can happen, and the guilt of the matter keeps us from talking. Eventually, we have to start back communicating, and when we do, the pride keeps us from addressing it. We would just converse as if nothing had happened at all. I squeezed out the excess water from the sponge as my cellular phone rang.

Taking off my gloves, I answered, "Hello?"

"Baby girl," my father spoke into the phone.

"Hey, Daddy."

"Another day out the office, huh?" he replied with a chuckle.

I had spent the last two days cleaning my father's properties because my house was spotless. He knew how I got when I had a lot on my mind. He didn't need to know about my pregnancy.

"Yes, I'm finishing up now. Almost time to get Cupcake from camp," I informed him.

"Shorty, you need to go ahead and invest in that housekeeping business like I told you," he preached.

He always insisted I invest in myself and start a cleaning company. I enjoyed cleaning and was the main person cleaning the properties.

After the accident, I had stepped back from being one of the top real estate agents. That night changed everything. Anxiety had taken over my life and being away from everyone became very comfortable for me. I became dynamic in running the office for my father, and then I started to clean the houses and properties.

"Maybe, Dad. I don't know. You know I just do it for relaxation," I told him as I walked to the window.

"Well, I just think it would be a great idea and investment. You could have your own office space and staff, and you'll already have a contract with me," he encouraged.

I looked out the window as I considered his offer. The view was breathtaking. The home had a sparkling Olympic-sized pool with a stunning waterfall surrounded by luscious evergreens, holly trees, oleanders, citrus trees, lavender, and lemongrass plants. It was an immaculate view. I took in the alluring landscape as I listened to the waterfall and my father preach. He was still on leave from work and home a lot. I'm sure that's where his motivation to push me was coming from.

I stepped outside to the backyard and took a seat by the lovely pool. "Uh-huh," I mumbled into the phone as my father continued to talk. This view was mesmerizing.

"Shorty, are you listening?" I heard my father speak.

"Yes, I hear you, Dad."

"Okay, I hope so. Come over this week, and we can talk more about it. I really want you to think about your future, baby girl. You have so much promised for you."

"I love you, Dad."

I could hear a woman mumbling in the background. "You got company, Daddy?" I inquired, being nosey.

"I'll call you later, baby girl. I love you more," he responded. Then quickly hung up the phone.

"Okay …" I said to myself as I closed my cellular phone. I took in the view a few more minutes. "I'm pregnant," I said to myself.

I was torn. I never thought I would have to consider the thought of an abortion again. I thought those days of my life were over. I couldn't imagine having another one. I aborted my first pregnancy because it was too soon. When I decided to give myself to C, I got pregnant the very first time. We were both too young for a baby. I was fresh out of high school, and C was busy with college and trade school. We both decided it was best.

Two years later came Cori, my sweet Cupcake. Life was perfect and beautiful. C was finishing with schooling and finally out the dope game. He started his business and charity, and everything was coming up. Then boom, eight months later I was pregnant again. I couldn't dare tell C we were expecting again so suddenly. Life was good for him. I'm certain he would've wanted to keep it, but I didn't want another baby.

I didn't want to be pregnant back-to-back, as he continued to succeed and travel. So, I secretly went and got another abortion.

Unfortunately, this pregnancy wasn't a secret anymore. I slipped up and told Jaz and Shay, and now C knew. However, I was still able to keep it away from Ryan. I was undecided on what to do. I was eight weeks pregnant and hiding it. The nauseated sensation and fatigue kept me lounged on the pool chair, and I eventually took a nap.

I woke up thirty minutes later, just in time to pick up my daughter from camp. I packed up my cleaning caddy and left the luxury home. I hopped into my Avalon and drove off to pick up my baby. I arrived at the summer camp shortly after. There stood my baby with her curly pigtails and pink bows. She stood laughing and playing with a couple girls her age. It always warmed my heart to see my baby smile and laugh. She was my soul.

She saw me pulling up, and the excitement matched her face. I pulled up alongside the sidewalk and reached over to unlock the door. She happily hopped in the passenger seat.

"Hey, Momma," she yelled.

"Hello, my love," I said to her as I reached over to kiss her cheek.

"I had so much fun today, Momma! Look at the bracelet I made," she said with pride. She held up her small wrist, and I examined her brightly colored yarn bracelet.

"It's beautiful, honey. You have got to make me one tomorrow," I told her with a smile.

"I sure will, Momma," she promised. She continued to tell me all about her day at summer camp. I had a surprise to stop by and rent a movie for us to watch that night. My birthday was approaching, but I just wanted to spend it with my baby girl at home. We pulled up to Blockbuster, and Cupcake got excited.

"Yay! Blockbuster! Let's get *The Little Mermaid*, Momma, and popcorn and chocolate," she said loudly as she got out of the car.

We walked into the store and went through the aisles and aisles of videocassettes. Cupcake picked up at least three princess movies and one horror movie she promised she was big enough to see. We got the movies, popcorn, and a few boxes of candy to accompany our movie night in. We checked out and headed home to start our quality time.

We got home, and I went to check the answering machine. No one had called but my father. I was surprised I hadn't heard from Ryan. I proceeded to go into the kitchen to start on dinner.

"Momma, I want to help you with dinner tonight," Cupcake told me as she followed me into the kitchen.

"Please do, baby. Come on, let me get your apron," I told her as I opened the pantry door for our aprons. "Here, now get your stool, wash up, and let's get ready to cook," I announced in a playful tone.

She laughed and ran to the sink to wash her little hands. I raided the refrigerator to see what was unfrozen to cook. "Chicken or burgers?" I quizzed my baby.

"Cheeseburgers," she answered with her arms up in the air.

"Cheeseburgers it is," I said as I pulled out the ground beef.

I let her help me make the burger patties. I enjoyed cooking with my daughter and teaching her new things.

"Always remember to clean while you cook, Cupcake," I told her as I handed her a towel to wipe down her area. We finished making our patties, and I cut up some potatoes for french fries. Cupcake pulled apart lettuce, and I sliced up a tomato. I also decided to sauté some onions.

"Oh, Momma, it smells so good," Cupcake said as she watched me cook the onions.

"It's going to taste even better because we made it together, sweetheart."

We finished making dinner and sat at the table to eat. We topped our burgers with all the fixings, and Cupcake drowned her fries in ketchup.

"Momma, what do you want for your birthday?" she asked me as she stuffed her face with a fry.

"I don't know, baby. I know I want to spend it with you."

She smiled with glee. "Oh, Momma! We can go to One Stop, and they can sing you 'Happy Birthday,' and we can play games," she gushed.

I chuckled at the idea of spending my birthday in a kid-friendly entertainment restaurant. "That sounds like a very good idea, Cupcake," I told her as I took a huge bite of my burger.

"Yep! TeTe Jaz and Shay can come. Pawpaw and Daddy! Uncle Trail! Maybe Ryan," she announced loudly.

I laughed at her guest list. "Okay, baby. Finish up, and we can watch some movies," I told her as I got up to clean my plate.

Cupcake finished her plate, and we loaded the dishwasher together.

"Momma, let's watch *The Little Mermaid* first, then we'll watch *Lion King*," she ordered as we left out the kitchen. Cupcake stretched out on the living room floor as I gathered the videocassettes. I popped in the movie and copped a seat on the carpet with my baby. As the previews rolled in, I reached over and began to tickle Cupcake.

"Mommyyyyyy," she screamed in the middle of laughter.

"I got you, I got you," I repeated as I covered her in kisses and tickles.

The movie played along, and so did we.

"Let me get the candy and pop the popcorn," I told her as I got up to collect the movie goodies.

I came back to the living room with a big bowl of warm popcorn. Cupcake had already found the candy and was snacking on it. We sat on the couch, and she snuggled up under me as we finished the last half of the movie. Cupcake drifted off by the time the credits were rolling. I laid her down softly as I crept up to run her a quick bath. She was cranky as I quickly got her in and out the tub and into her pajamas.

"Good night, Mommy," she whispered as she got comfortable in her bed.

"Good night, my sweet Cupcake." I kissed her forehead, turned on her lamp, and left her bedroom.

I went back to the living room to straighten up our mess. I felt a nauseous feeling as I bent down to pick up toys. I immediately ran to the restroom to vomit. I kneeled against the toilet and threw up everything I had eaten that evening. I had to catch my breath as I stood up. I washed my face and swished some mouthwash around my mouth.

I finished cleaning the living room and decided to run myself a bubble bath. I lit a few candles in my bathroom and turned on some soft music. I poured my aromatherapy bubble bath under the hot running water. Then there was a knock followed by my doorbell ringing. I looked at the clock on the wall and saw that it was 9:10 p.m. I went to answer the door, wondering who it could be. I opened the door, and there stood Ryan.

"Hey, boo," he greeted and pulled me into his arms.

"Hey," I mumbled against his neck.

He pulled away and looked at me. "You look beautiful as always."

"Thank you. What … What are you doing here?" I asked.

"Well, I was in the neighborhood and thought I'd stop by. And … I have your birthday present," he told me as he walked past me into my house.

I closed and locked the door as I watched him enter with a huge smile. "What? Ryan, what are you talking about? Where is it?"

"I know you haven't been talking much about your birthday, but I was thinking," he said as he pulled me to him. He began to place kisses on my cheek and neck. "Maybe … You, me, and Cupcake can take a trip to paradise for your birthday. Take your mind off whatever has been occupying it," he offered with sweet kisses.

"Wait … What are you saying?" I asked again.

He then pulled three airline tickets out of his back pocket. I snatched them from him with excitement. I gazed them over to see where he was trying to take us.

"Jamaica?!" I screamed.

"Yes, babe. Just us for a few days. On a beautiful island with my beautiful girls," he replied.

Wow. I couldn't believe he had this planned. "But I have work, and Cupcake has camp," I proclaimed.

"It's just for a few days, Sydney. The weekend is coming up. You'll just have to take off tomorrow and Monday. We leave in the morning," he told me as he pulled me close.

I then begin to kiss him. I kissed him deeply as I caressed his face. That kiss led us to the bedroom. As we approached the bedroom, I heard the bath water that I'd completely forgotten about.

"Oh, Ryan," I yelled as I ran to my bathroom.

Water and bubbles were everywhere. I quickly ran to the tub to turn the water off. I looked up, and Ryan was standing in the doorway laughing.

"This is not funny," I told him, trying to throw bubbles at him.

"Yes, it really is," he chuckled, throwing bubbles at me.

"Do not start, Ryan," I warned, standing to throw more at him. Before I knew it, we were throwing bubbles and on the floor wrestling. Laughter and bubbles filled my bathroom. It was times like this that were making me fall for Ryan.

He had me pinned against the rug on the bathroom floor. I looked up to him, admiring his handsomeness. He began to kiss me softly, and I reciprocated. He let my arms free, and I wrapped them around his neck. He used his hands to caress my curves as he touched my body. I fell into his kisses, and my body jerked to his touch. The bathroom floor was wet, and so were our clothes. He pulled away from kissing me and sat up to take off his shirt.

Lord, is Ryan sexy, I thought. I could feel him between my legs, and I wanted him. I wanted to feel him inside me. He kissed on my neck and nibbled on my collarbone, which drove me crazy. I knew he loved how I squirmed in his arms from his lips and tongue. I ran my fingertips up and down his back. He started to take off my shirt to reveal my 36 Cs in a sexy satin bra. He then unfastened my bra to suck and lick my nipples with sincerity. Ryan knew how to suck my breasts. They were so sensitive lately, yet he was so delicate.

"Oh my God," I expressed as he continued to suck my breasts.

He grabbed both and pushed them together as he attempted to suck both nipples. I kissed his forehead as he continued to pleasure me. He began to kiss his way down. His lips and tongue felt so good against my stomach. He started to take off my pants and underwear. I laid naked on top of the wet rug, surrounded by bubbles. Ryan laid down against the floor and initiated to kiss my thighs. He was so sensual. He bit and licked on my thighs, satisfying me and making me want more. He then softly kissed my pussy, and I jumped at the feel of his lips against my lips. He opened his mouth and spread my legs wider.

"Yes," I gasped. My words then turned into moans. I couldn't hold it any longer, and I was climaxing within minutes. My body embarked on its usual uncontrollable shake.

"You all right, sweetie?" he asked as he slipped off his pants and into the condom.

I could barely move. I couldn't answer him, and he knew it. He slid back in between my legs and then into my wet pussy. He kissed me deeply as he slowly entered inside of me. Ryan took it slow and easy. The bubbles everywhere, the candles, and the music had me in a trance. Ryan knew how to make love. Literally. I could feel that he felt something about me by the way he touched me, kissed me, made love to me. The candles were burned out by the time we finished. We laid on the bathroom rug with heavy and fast breathing. I laid under him, wrapped in his arms.

"Thank you, baby," he stated as he looked me in my eyes.

"What are you thanking me for?" I asked, curious.

"For making me feel so good. Thank you," he repeated as he kissed the top of my head.

We laid on the floor a little bit longer before we got up to shower. I had to pack Cupcake and I luggage before I went to sleep. Ryan had our flight booked the very next morning.

CHAPTER 12

Shit. I couldn't believe I forgot the film for the Polaroid camera.

"Ride with me to the store, boo," I told Evelyn as she passed out popsicles.

It was a beautiful Saturday, and today was our Fourth Annual Old Skool vs. New Skool Basketball Tournament. It was a school supply fundraiser that Trail, and I started with our charity, The World Is Yours Foundation. We held the event at our community center every year.

All the old cats who thought they still had game would go against the up-and-coming high school basketball stars. Everyone in the hood would participate, volunteer, and attend. The city respected what we were accomplishing. This year we decided to have the tournament outside. The weather was perfect, and the event was going great.

My daughter was gone with her mother for an unexpected birthday trip, so I asked Evelyn to accompany me to my event. She agreed and even sponsored a few items.

"Okay, let me pass out this last batch," she replied as she handed the eager children frozen treats.

The park and parking lot were full. I looked around and appreciated that everyone was enjoying themselves, smiling, laughing, and having fun.

"Trail, I'll be back, homie! 'Bout to head to the store real quick," I yelled to him.

He looked over, nodded, and continued to coach. Evelyn promised the children she would be back, hugged them, and then grabbed my hand.

"Looks like you're having fun," I commented as we walked to my car.

"I am. C, this is so nice! I love what you guys are doing here. It's amazing," she told me, smiling.

She was beautiful. She had her long, black hair in a high ponytail. She wore our logo T-shirt with a pair of blue jean shorts. Her legs and body were toned and slender.

"Thank you," I replied.

We reached my old-school, candy-coated whip. I only brought this beauty out on special occasions. Plus, it was a habit for me to ride my 1966 Pontiac Catalina to the hood.

"Okay, so this is your whip?" Evelyn asked, walking around the car. "You clean, C! I see ya! Electric pearl blue with the flakes, cocaine white and blue stitch interior, twenty-inch gold vouges and bows, white walls, gold grill! Okay then," she yelled, jokingly.

"You don't know nothing 'bout that, Doctor," I playfully told her.

"Just as you have layers, so do I," she declared.

I reached for her door, and she slid into the passenger seat. She even leaned over and unlocked my door. Noted. I got into the car and grabbed my cd case.

"I'll DJ. You drive," Evelyn told me as she took the booklet from my hands.

I smiled at her. "Dig that," I replied as I drove off the lot. I stopped by the nearest pharmacy. I got back into the car and filled the back seat with my purchase of film and disposable cameras.

As I was pulling out of the lot, Evelyn asked, "So did you grow up around here?"

I chuckled. "Yeah, you want to see where?"

"Yes! I would love to!"

"Okay." I switched my blinker and took her on the journey through my old stomping grounds. I pointed out all the walkways we took to and from school and showed her where I had my first fistfight. We rode past my high school. I showed her all the spots I used to post up at. I even showed her our corner store, which was a vital vein in any hood.

"Okay, right there. That duplex there," I showed her. We pulled up in front of my childhood home.

"Oh, wow. So, you grew up here? You and your sister?" she asked.

"Yes. And Momma. But yeah, this is where it all started for me. Hustling these same streets, I grew up on. But now I'm more interested in buying the streets."

She looked at me. She then leaned over and kissed me. Her lips were soft against mine as I kissed her back.

She pulled away and stated, "It's just so refreshing seeing a man, a black man, so passionate about uplifting and owning his own neighborhood."

"Thank you, boo. I owe a lot to Trail, though. He was very instrumental in my life," I expressed to her.

She continued to listen to me as she looked around the empty neighborhood. Almost everyone was at the tournament. We'd made sure of it because we always sent shuttle buses to the hood.

"Thanks again for coming with me to this event," I told her as I started the car.

"You are more than welcome. I feel honored to sponsor and accompany you, Mr. Stone," she told me very sexily.

I looked over to her, and she gave me a look. Maybe it was the beautiful summer day, or maybe she was feeling me more so than ever. We pulled back up to the park, and my reserved space was still empty. I backed in and parked my wet painted whip. I exited the car with the bags full of film and cameras.

It was packed. Brightly colored vintage vehicles took up most spaces. This was an event for everyone to bring out their pride and joy on rims. Barbecue and weed smoke filled the air. Bubbles flew in the wind, as music pumped in the background. Evelyn reached for my hand as we walked over to the park benches. They were painting faces and passing out stickers. My homie Wiz sponsored a few of his girls to help with everything.

"I'll get the camera and get a few pictures," Evelyn told me as she reached for the film.

"Thanks, boo. Let me go holla at Trail for a minute. I'll be right back," I informed her.

"Heyyy, C," a group of women said in unison.

I smiled and waved as they continued to walk past. Evelyn reached up on her tiptoes to kiss me in the corner of the lips. I laughed to myself as I walked off. I could feel her subtly letting other women know she was with me—that she was my woman for the event. I found it funny.

I was never public with any other woman besides Shorty. The hood had never seen me with a chick like that. Shorty and my relationship was the only relationship I had been in. Well, I experienced puppy love in junior high, but I met Shorty shortly after high school.

I could remember laying eyes on her for the first time. She was walking home from school with her friends, and she stood completely out. Her beautiful curly brown hair and light brown eyes were captivating. She was so young and so beautiful. Her body was perfect. I saw her and knew I had to have her. I was willing to wait as long as it took, but I would eventually get her. And I did.

I now looked back over our relationship and figured maybe we were too young. Maybe we were too naive. Maybe we were too stubborn. I guess we would never know because it ended how it did. I still felt guilt over the whole situation. My pride never allowed me talk to her about that night. Sometimes I thought back to how it would've been if we would have just communicated—discussed why she did it. I tried not to blame her solely, even though I knew I'd done everything right. I never cheated on Shorty—ever.

I found out later Duke was in her ear, planting bugs and lies. No man had the balls or audacity to approach Shorty when we were together. Niggas knew who I was and how I got down. However, the person closest to me had the boldness to get at my woman behind my back. I provided for her and our family. I protected them. I once had a crazy thought that Shorty and I could get back together and work things out, but as time continued to pass, that thought became a faded dream. Now it was time to turn the page and make amends.

I reached the court where Trail was coaching New Skool. He was on the sideline talking to the ref.

"C! What up, nigga?" I could hear my homeboy yell from across the court.

I threw the peace sign as I approached Trail. "Wut up, dog?"

"Shit, shit. Everything good?" he asked.

"Oh yeah. I just had to go get more cameras and film for the

Polaroid. I think we got about fifty backpacks already," I told him proudly.

The event had a good turnout. Everyone was donating money, school supplies, clothes, and books.

"Yeah! I saw that. I think the pot was at about $7,388.09 last I checked. This year is better than last," he said with a huge smile.

I was grateful to have someone like Trail to look up to. You get more when you give. That was his motto. The true art of giving and receiving was universal law for me. My life was the epitome of that.

"I see your lady is really enjoying herself," he stated, looking in her direction.

"Yeah. You know I hate CC not here with me, but hey … I'm feeling Evelyn. She a boss. She sexy as hell. Smart. She's very good with kids and passionate about giving back as well."

"Right. Tell her I said thanks for all the skin supplies. I'm going to put them in the backpacks for the teenagers!"

My cell phone then rang. "Hold up," I told him as I walked off. "C," I greeted.

"You have a collect call from … Shorty," I could hear from the other end "To accept, press 1 to …"

I quickly interrupted the recording and pressed 1.

"Hello?" I could hear Shorty say from the other end.

"Shorty, what's up?! Happy Birthday, love," I told her.

"Thank you, C," I could hear her smiling through her teeth.

"So, are you enjoying your birthday?" I asked, curious. I found it strange she was calling me while on a birthday vacation with her man, but life is strange.

"Yes! I really am. Oh my gosh, C. It's so freaking pretty here. The water is so blue and crystal clear. The sky and the beautiful palm trees. The sun looks like it shines different here," she told me with a laugh.

"Dig that. Sounds as beautiful as you. Where my baby at?"

"Her and Ryan went to go swim. I wasn't feeling too good, so I decided to stay behind."

"Oh, yeah. That's right."

"What's that supposed to mean, C?" she asked defensively.

"Nothing. I forgot about your little situation."

"So that's what you're calling it?"

"Well what are you calling it?"

"I don't even want to talk about that. What you got me for my birthday," she deflected.

"Exactly. But yeah, I got you something. It's a surprise."

"You know I don't like surprises," she replied. "Mommy! Mommy! We're back," I could hear my daughter yell in the background.

"Let me talk to her," I told Shorty.

"Okay, hold on," she responded as she placed the receiver down.

Moments later, my baby girl picked up the phone. "Daddy! I miss you," my baby yelled into the receiver.

"I miss you too, baby! I wish you were here with me at the park for the basketball tournament."

"I do too, Daddy. Guess what?! I went swimming, Daddy! I had so much fun," she announced.

"I'm glad you're having fun, baby."

She began to tell me all about her day of swimming and hunting for seashells. "Daddy, I got you some seashells too," she gladly said.

"Thank you, baby. I can't wait to see them. I want you to have fun, so you can tell me all about it when you get home. I love you. Put your mom back on the phone."

"Okay. Love you too, Daddy. Hold on!" She ran off to find her mom.

"Hello," a voice said into the phone. It was a man, so I'm certain it was that lame, Ryan. "Hello," he stated again.

"Yeah," I spit into the receiver.

He chuckled and went on, "Oh, it's you. You calling my Sydney to wish her a happy birthday, huh?! I'd appreciate it if you would just stay away from my woman, bro."

I barely listened to his harmless threat. "Homie, you do know I have no clue where you and yo' woman at, right? Maybe you should have a conversation with your woman about staying away from me," I replied.

His chuckle abruptly stopped. He was quiet for a while. "I know you probably upset that she's moving on, but get over it. She's mine now," he told me with his idea of authority.

Hilarious, I thought. "Yet, you're on the phone with me. Your woman called me. Check your woman, *bro*. Peace," I told him and hung up the phone.

I turned around, and Evelyn was walking up to me. I pulled her to me and kissed her deeply. She wrapped her arms tightly around my neck as she kissed me with just as much passion.

"Get a room. There are kids here," I heard someone jokingly judge as they walked pass.

Evelyn pulled away and looked me deeply in my eyes. "What was that for?"

"Nothing. You just look so damn good."

The day went on great. The New Skool team won the tournament. All the d-boys came through and supported tremendously. The evening was winding down, and the sun was beginning to set. Trail had everyone meet around in the court. I was the front man for the company, charity, and, later, all major dope transactions. Trail handed me the mike, and I did what I do.

"Wut up, everybody?! I just want to thank each one of you for coming through with your support and energy. Tomorrow night is the talent show and giveaway. I hope you can all come out just one more time to support. Tomorrow's event is free! Everyone who has already signed up and auditioned for the talent show will perform. No last-minute acts—no exceptions! Anyway, today was epic! Let's continue to support, encourage, and love one another. Good night, y'all." I spoke as the entire crowd broke into a round of applause. I exited the center of attention and grabbed Evelyn by the hand as we disappeared in the crowd.

"We did it again, homie," Trail exclaimed as we slapped hands.

"That we did, man. That we did," I replied proudly.

"You and your lady can bounce. We got this," Trail told me as he passed me a stuffed blunt.

"You sure, man?" I responded as I hit the blunt.

"Yeah! Enjoy your night, and I'll call you in the morning."

We slapped fives, and Evelyn and I proceeded to the car. "So … Am I trailing you to your house or …" Evelyn stated.

It stopped me in my tracks. I could feel her vibe, and I was digging it. "Yeah. I'm closer, so it could be convenient if we go to my crib. If you don't feel like driving, I can get your car to my house," I told her as I looked down to her.

"Okay. But what do you mean you can get my car to your house?" she quizzed.

I looked around the parking lot. I saw one of the young cats who ran for me. "Aye, P! P! Come here and let me holla at ya," I yelled.

He was talking to some chick, but once he realized it was me calling for him, he immediately ran over. "C, wut's up? You good?" he asked, almost out of breath.

"Yeah, I'm good. I need you to get a car to my house. I trust you can do that," I instructed.

"Yeah! You know I got you, big homie!"

I asked Evelyn for her keys. Of course, she was a bit unconvinced at first. I took the keys from her and directed the young buck on what to do. He nodded in accordance as Evelyn and I slid into my convertible.

"So, you still the man in the hood, huh? I see I had that part right," Evelyn stated as we rode the streets.

I chuckled at her. "I'm well respected. There's a difference. You see, I do a lot for the hood. I love the hood, and the hood loves me."

I reached over and grabbed her hand to kiss the back of it. I was really feeling Evelyn. I really enjoyed today with her. She was everything I wanted in a woman. I felt like I wanted her to be my woman. Shorty being pregnant and getting me involved with this maybe baby daddy bullshit was insane. I didn't want to play along with Shorty's games anymore. I was ready to find someone for me—maybe even take a shot at real love again.

Evelyn got the CD book and put in an old-school R&B group. The powerful love ballad blasted through the twelve-inch speakers. We pulled up at my house, and she was in awe.

"Whoa. Your home is beautiful," she stated, walking to the doorway.

"Thanks. I built this about five years ago. Come on in," I proclaimed, opening the huge mahogany front doors. I set the keys on the credenza in the foyer.

She stepped inside and looked up to the high vaulted ceilings and crystal chandeliers. I could tell she was truly admiring my home.

"Oh, wow," she stated as she walked to the painting over my

fireplace in the living room. It was a huge painting of a breathtaking sunset or sunrise, depending on how you looked at it. "I love this piece! The sun looks like its shining," she declared.

"Do you see a sunset or sunrise?" I asked, curious.

"It's a sunset," she told me. "Why? What do you see?"

"It's a sunrise, I think," I replied as I pulled her to me and kissed her. "I got some clothes you can change in if you want to take a shower or bath," I offered.

"Yes, please. Thank you, C," she replied.

I then led her to the guest bedroom down the hall. I went to get her towels and a fresh sweat suit. "I'll be in the den if you need anything," I told her as I exited the room. I went to sit on the couch and turn on the TV. I put it on the sports channel to catch up on the recent highlights.

After all the blunts and beers, I still felt a little buzzed. Only minutes had passed before I could feel Evelyn watching me. I turned around, and there she was—naked in the doorway.

"I think I will need you to wash my back," she informed me.

Those words immediately made me erect and horny. Her body was flawless and unblemished. She had bubbles scattered here and there. I wanted to kiss her everywhere they weren't.

"I don't want to walk over and track up your floors, but I want you, C," she told me. The tone of her voice let me know what was up.

I walked over to her and picked her up. We began to kiss deeply as we kissed our way to the bedroom downstairs. We arrived in the guest bathroom, and she had the entire tub filled with bubbles. I set her on the counter as I kissed on her long, sexy neck. She pierced her fingernails into my back as I teased her neck with kisses. She began to take off my shirt and help unbuckle my belt.

"Damn," she mumbled as she looked at my chest and abs. She ran her hands over my torso as she licked her lips.

I pulled out my wallet and found a condom. She jumped off the countertop and onto her knees. I was surprised she was so quick to please me. She pulled out my dick and stuffed her mouth with it. She sucked him softly and slowly at first. As she continued, she got so into it, and I couldn't conceal my moans. She deep-throated my dick, as he disappeared into her mouth. She used both hands to stroke him, as her mouth sucked and applied lubricant. I could feel the pleasure she took in pleasing me. I was stimulated and ready to penetrate her. Before I could break away from the fellatio, she made me bust in her mouth.

"Oh shit," I abruptly yelled. I was cuming, and she was still sucking. I was in heaven. I had a hand full of her thick, black hair.

She then rose from her knees and kissed my cheek. "Come on, wash my back," she instructed as she led me to the bubble-filled tub.

CHAPTER 13

It felt so good to be back in my city. I was anticipating diving into my comfortable queen-sized bed, as we drove to my house. I enjoyed my trip and my twenty-seventh birthday. Ryan showered me in gifts and love while in paradise. We pulled into my neighborhood, and I could see something bright red near my front yard. I sat up, and so did Ryan, as we pulled closer.

It was a shiny silver, brand-new Lexus GS300 parked in my driveway, accompanied by a huge red bow. I smiled so hard as Ryan parked his car. Cupcake was still asleep on the back seat as I hopped out the car. I walked around the vehicle in awe.

"Did your dad get you this?" Ryan asked as he looked inside the car.

"I don't know. He hasn't told me what he got me yet."

"There's a note in there," he told me, opening the door.

I walked over to get the note. I slid into the luxury leather seats. *Shorty* was handwritten on the front of the note. I smiled, recognizing the handwriting.

"Keys under the driver's mat. Hope this is your best birthday yet. Happy Birthday, Love. … C."

I beamed from ear to ear.

"What does it say?" Ryan quizzed.

It smelled of new car. The leather smelled so good. I looked around the interior of the beautiful car—wood grain, CD player, mirror tint. It felt like my very first car. Ryan took the note from my hands as I delighted in my new whip.

"What the fuck?! C gave you this car?! Oh no! You're giving this back to him," Ryan demanded.

"What? What are you talking about, Ryan?" I asked, getting out.

"Why would he give you such an extravagant gift, Sydney? Is there anything you need to tell me?" Ryan inquired with a piercing stare.

"What?! Ryan, that is the father of my child! We are not doing this, and I'm not giving that car back. I'm about to get my baby and go inside my house," I announced as I turned to walk away from him.

He grabbed me by my arm and roared, "Sydney! Don't ever walk away from me again! Talk to me! Tell me what's going on between you two!"

It was a Tuesday morning, and luckily, no one was outside. I could only hope the neighbors weren't peeking through the blinds.

"Ryan, let go of me," I demanded as I pushed him off me. I couldn't believe his behavior and jealousy. I wasn't accustomed to dating a jealous man. C was very confident. I wasn't familiar with possessiveness or obsession, and it was starting to get on my nerves. "Ryan, you should go home," I told him as I walked to his car.

"Sydney, I'm sorry. I didn't mean to overreact like that. Sydney," he called as I got Cupcake out the back seat.

I was silent as I carried my baby to the front door. *She is getting heavier by the day*, I thought. I unlocked the doors and laid her on the sofa in the living room. I exited to go get the rest of our belongings, and Ryan met me on the porch.

"Here," he stated, as he handed me our bags.

"Thank you."

Silence approached us.

"Sydney ... Hey, I'm sorry. I'm just really into you. I love you. I don't want nothing or no one to come between us," he told me with puppy-dog eyes.

It was strange because it felt like he really did love me. However, I knew I didn't love him. I'd felt love before, and I knew this wasn't it. I liked him. I enjoyed time we spent together. But I wasn't in love.

"Ryan, love works both ways. I'm really digging you and our vibe, but I can't stand here and honestly tell you I love you or that I'm in love," I spoke.

"I know it's early, but, Sydney, I really feel like you are the one. I was out of line for grabbing you. I sincerely apologize. But when I feel like I have to compete with someone you have a child with, a past with, and now luxurious gifts, how am I supposed to feel?" he asked.

I was quiet.

"I'll leave and give you some time to breathe and relax. But understand this, Sydney: I'm only here to love you, not hurt you. You are the best thing that has ever happened to me. Happy birthday again, baby," he told me and walked off.

I stood there and watched him in get into his car and drive off. I put the bags in the house and walked to check the mailbox. Of course, there were only bills and a couple magazines. I looked around my neighborhood as I walked back up the driveway to my house. I didn't know what to think of Ryan's behavior. I couldn't believe he would demand that I give the car back. I was positively not doing that.

I entered my house and locked the storm door. My baby was sleeping peacefully on the couch. Her curly brown hair was all over her head. I sat next to her and began to push her hair out of her adorable face. It was quiet in my home. I kicked off my shoes and began to browse through the magazine. Halfway through the booklet, my pager went off. It was C. I reached over and grabbed the telephone to call him.

"C," he answered.

"Hey, C," I spoke into the receiver. "Thank you soooo much for the car! It's so freaking pretty," I exclaimed.

"You welcome. I was just hitting you up to make sure you guys made it back safely. What my baby doing?" he asked.

"She's napping."

"Oh, okay. I bought that car before y'all's lil trip was planned, just so you know," he informed me.

I snickered and replied, "It doesn't matter. It's perfect, and I love it! Thanks so much, C!"

"It's all good, Shorty. Call me when Cupcake wake up," he told me and then hung up.

I picked up my baby and held her in my arms as I got comfortable on the couch. She was still sleeping so peacefully. I snuggled up with her and decided to nap as well.

I was awakened from the ringing of the telephone. "Hello," I spoke into the receiver.

"Hey, girl! Welcome back! Happy birthday," Shay screamed into the phone.

I pulled the phone away from my ear with her screaming. "Hey! Thanks, girl," I replied.

"Happy birthday, Shorty," I heard Jaz squeak in the background.

"Thanks! What y'all doing?" I asked as I sat up on the sofa.

"Not much. Jaz stopped by the store. We just calling to make sure Ryan brought you and Cupcake back safe," Shay told me.

I chuckled and responded, "Yeah, he did. We really had a good time. Well, until we got back."

"Why? What happened?" Jaz asked in the background.

"Girl, we'll have to talk about that later over drinks ... well, dinner or something," I commented.

"Yes! Let's do that! Let's get together tonight for dinner. I know you're over the club scene, so let's have a nice fancy dinner, like old times! We need to catch up anyway," Shay suggested.

I contemplated the offer. Since we hadn't been clubbing, it did seem like awhile since my girls and I had kicked it. "Okay, we can do that. Where and what time?" I asked.

"Let's meet up at Notch 'round seven o'clock ... How's that?" she asked.

I looked over to the clock on the wall. It was only 12:12 p.m. "Yeah, that's perfect. Okay, see y'all later," I replied.

Our conversation was then ended. I woke up my baby girl from her peaceful sleep. She whined a bit as I sat her up on the couch. "Cupcake. Wake up, baby," I told her.

She wiped her precious eyes with her petite hands. "Mommy," she whined.

"Wake up, Cori," I playfully sang. "You gotta see the birthday present your Daddy got me," I told her.

She opened her big, bright eyes once I mentioned her father. He had that effect on us both. "Where?" she quizzed, looking around.

"It's outside. Let's go see Pawpaw too," I happily said.

She jumped up off the couch and ran to the front door. She could see the shiny new car and bright red bow through the door. "Mommy! It's a car! Mommy, lets drive in it! I want to sit in the front," she told me, reaching for the knob.

"Okay, hold on," I replied. I went to get my purse, beeper, and keys.

We exited the house, and she ran to the car. "Unlock the door, Mommy," she told me.

I unlocked the doors and took the huge bow off to put it on the back seat. We drove off, and I decided to stop by a drive-thru for a quick meal. We arrived at my father's shortly after. I knew he was home even though I didn't see his car. He had been released from the hospital weeks prior and was doing great on his recovery. Cupcake and I walked up to his massive entry doors. I rang the doorbell to let him know we were entering, but I used my key to gain entrance.

"Pawpaw," Cupcake yelled, running to give him a huge hug.

He was walking toward the foyer with his cane. It was different seeing my daddy in a handicapped state.

"Dad, sit down. We're in now," I told him.

"It's okay. I'm up now. I can walk, you know, Shorty."

"Okay, you got this," I replied. "Cupcake, go to the kitchen to eat your food, baby."

"Okay, Mommy … I missed you, Pawpaw," she stated, blowing him a kiss as she walked off.

"Welcome back, baby. Happy birthday. I had a feeling you were coming over here today," he declared, walking over to hug me.

I hugged him so tightly. I missed my daddy. "Thank you, Daddy," I replied.

"I'm sure you came over for your birthday gift, huh?" he stated, walking toward the family room.

"Actually, no. I missed you. I decided to stop by instead of calling. And … I might need you to watch Cupcake for a few hours," I answered him. I sat on the sofa.

He had all the blinds open and a few windows. The sun shined beautifully into the room. He reached for a wrapped box from the fireplace mantle. It was wrapped in fancy, brightly colored wrapping paper with matching bows.

"Oh, Dad," I exclaimed.

He slowly took a seat on the recliner. "Open it," he rushed me.

I unwrapped the perfectly wrapped gift in excitement. It was a box filled with documents and a blank check in the amount of ten thousand dollars. I looked over the documents. It was a business plan for starting a housekeeping company.

"As you can see, I went ahead and got the first step done for you. That is a detailed and thorough business plan. The money is just an investment from me to you for your birthday. I left it blank because it's your decision how to name your company. I believe in you, Shorty. It's time to take your future seriously. I love you, and I'm always here to support you."

We sat and talked for a couple hours. Cupcake came in to take over the television, while we continued to catch up. I didn't disclose to him the episode from earlier. I didn't want my father to worry. Plus, I knew Ryan would never harm me. I still hadn't told my father I was pregnant. I knew I couldn't hide it forever, but I was still unsure of the whole thing.

"Well, Dad, I should get going so I can go home and get ready," I announced as I stood up.

"Let me walk you to your new car so I can check it out," he suggested.

"Okay. Cupcake, baby, I'll be back later to get you. Spend some time with Pawpaw. You can tell him all about the trip," I told her as I bent down to hug her. I embraced her tightly and kissed her chubby cheek. "Love you, mommy's sweet Cupcake," I commented.

My father walked me to my car and admired the decked-out automobile. "C did good. You got a CD player! This is a sweet ride, Shorty," he stated, looking at the interior.

"Yeah, he's awesome," I admitted.

"Well, enjoy your birthday dinner and tell your friends I said hello," my dad spoke right before I drove off.

I opened the sunroof and enjoyed the breeze and the last of the sunlight before it began to set. I turned the volume up on the radio to the max for the rest of my ride. Once I made it into the house, I was immediately nauseous. I ran to the bathroom to quickly vomit. The morning sickness lasted through the afternoon and evening.

This pregnancy was going to be different, I thought. I looked at my reflection in the mirror. I was imagining myself with a round belly and wide nose. I swished a capful of mouthwash around my mouth before I exited the bathroom. I walked to my bedroom and into my closet to find something sexy to wear. I decided to slip into a bold, abstract print Versace dress. The colors were eye-catching, and it would fit my body like glove.

I ran my bath water and took a quick bath. I wanted enough time to do my makeup and crimp my hair. I finished up and slipped into a strappy red pair of Jimmy Choo heels. Ryan had bought me a gold and diamond-encrusted bracelet and matching necklace. I added the pieces to complete my look as I grabbed my classic red, quilted Chanel bag. I looked and felt gorgeous. I sprayed my favorite scent, Chanel No. 5, on before I left my bedroom. I grabbed my cellular phone before I left my house.

I rode to the fine dining restaurant feeling fine. I pulled up to the establishment, and the valet was there to open my door.

"Nice ride," he told me, helping me out the car.

"Thanks," I replied, handing him a tip.

I walked into the restaurant and was sat at our reserved table. The restaurant was impeccable. The setting was so soft and romantic.

"Good evening, madam. I am Mark, and I will be your server for the evening. Please, let me take your drink order," he announced as he poured me a glass of water with lemon.

"I'm waiting on my two friends. I'm sure once they make it, we'll have champagne," I reported.

He nodded and walked off. Shortly after, my two best friends arrived with gift bags. They looked stunning in their jaw-dropping evening attire. Shay had on a sleeveless hot pink dress with a sexy neckline. It fit her tight at the waistline and pleated out at the lower waist and hip. She had on six-inch purple stilettos, and her hair was in a long fishbone braid to the side. Jaz was giving off a Janet Jackson I-get-so-lonely look in her black, fitted dress pants and white button-up shirt. She had a few buttons left undone, revealing her sexy lace bra and plump cleavage. Her heels were tall, and her hair was long and wavy. She even had the sexy fedora to complete the look.

I stood up to hug my friends.

"Shorty! Happy birthday," they both said.

"Girl, you fine! Jamaica did you good," Shay gushed as she looked me up and down. We sat down and immediately began our chitchat. I had to update them on all the gifts from all the men in my life.

"Wait ... So, you got a surprise trip to paradise, jewelry, clothes, a brand-new whip, and a business?! Cheers to you, Shorty! This is your year, baby," Jaz stated aloud, raising her glass to toast.

I only took a couple sips of champagne for the night. "Yeah, but it's not all that good. Let's not forget I'm pregnant by I don't know whom. I'm torn between two men. And Ryan kind of spazzed out on me earlier today because of C buying me that car."

"I'm sure he did," Shay mumbled as she and Jaz broke out in laughter.

"I'm serious, you guys. He wanted me to give the car back to C," I told them as I took a bite of my food.

"Oh no, he should know you're not going to do that," Jaz replied.

"Yeah, he thinks something is going on with me and C."

"I feel him. What is going on with you and C?" Shay asked as she sipped her champagne. "Hell, what's going on with you and Ryan?!"

We all laughed at her comment. I began to think about my now-complicated love life. As time continued to go on, I began to accept the fact of having another baby. I would just deal with the outcome when it arrived.

"Now that's where I'm totally confused, y'all. I think I'm going to call C once I leave here, maybe see if I can swing through," I admitted with a small blush.

"Yeah, make sure you don't pop up over his house anymore unannounced," Jaz chuckled.

I cut my eyes at her but joined in on the laughter. It felt good to talk to my friends in a judge-free zone, to laugh at my problems for a minute instead of stressing over them, and to openly speak my issues and know they wouldn't judge me one bit. It was a good feeling to be surrounded by people who genuinely loved and encouraged me.

We enjoyed our spectacular dinner. I opted out on drinking, while they enjoyed cosmos and convos for the remainder of the evening.

"Okay, we need to see this car," Shay broadcast.

We got up to exit the restaurant and waited for the valet to recover our vehicles. We joked around while we waited on our cars. Shay flirted with the young valet.

"You sure you don't want to go to the club and floss tonight, Shorty? Hell, we look damn good," Jaz proclaimed.

It was a nice idea. I really did feel like flossing. I was feeling myself. But I was over the club scene.

"Nah, I'm gone, y'all! Thanks so much for dinner and the gifts. I love you guys so much. My soul sisters," I declared as we all hugged.

Jaz rode off with Shay. I hopped into my car and decided to call C before I pulled off.

"C," he answered.

"Hey, C."

"Shorty. What's up?"

"Oh, nothing. Just calling to see if you were busy. I wanted to ... maybe stop by. Say thank you for the gift," I suggested. I was smiling and hoping he would say yes. I was still a bit pissed at Ryan, and I wanted C to see how good I was looking. I wanted him to see me and want me.

"Yeah ... I'm kind of tied up right now," he stated.

"Carleon, you're going to miss the best part! I'm not rewinding either," I heard some chick say in the background.

I felt my heart sink to the bottom of my feet. Silence crept upon us. "I guess I'll let you go. Enjoy your night, Carleon," I replied.

Our conversation was then ended. I saw in that moment that C had really moved on. I saw that the car really didn't mean anything. That passionate night didn't mean anything. Me pouring my heart out meant nothing. I rode to get my daughter from my dad's and was happy that we made it home quickly. I lit some candles in my bedroom and put on some R&B music. My pager then went off. It was Ryan. I decided to answer his page.

"Hello," he answered.

"Hey," I replied.

"Sydney. Hello. I'm so glad you decided to call," he said so sincerely.

"What's up?" I spit back.

"Nothing. I was just missing you and checking on you. You know, I didn't mean any harm earlier …" he went on, "but you mean a lot to me. I understand you cannot honestly say the same thing right now, and that's okay. I know we will be happy and in love one day, Sydney. You are the one. You're my one. You are beautiful, smart, funny, and perfect. I'll wait as long as I have to for you."

It warmed my heart to think and feel that he cared for me so much. Even though I didn't have the love I wanted from C, Ryan was willing to give me that and more.

"I hear you, Ryan. I just need you to be patient with me," I stated.

"I will, baby. I promise. I will be patient. You are worth it."

"Thank you. Why don't you come over tomorrow? I have something to tell you," I spit out.

"What?! What is it Sydney? Is everything okay," he inquired, concerned.

"Yes, everything is fine. We just need to talk," I told him.

"Okay. Well, I'll see you tomorrow, Sydney. Sweet dreams, beautiful," he told me and then hung up the phone.

I meditated for half an hour before I decided to finally call it a night. Things were happening and changing in my life. It was up to me to accept it for better or worse. Either way, it was my decision because it was my life.

CHAPTER 14

Shit. Who the fuck calling me now?! I thought. I had just hung up the phone with Shorty, trying to get back to movie night with Evelyn. I came into my living room to take the call while Evelyn waited patiently for me in the den. I wondered if she was calling back to demand I allow her to come over. Shorty had been so out of character lately—just didn't seem to be acting like herself.

I answered the phone roughly, "Yeah, wut's up?!"

"Uh, yeah ... is this C?" the person inquired from the other end.

"Who is this?" I said to the unfamiliar voice.

"This is Ryan, Sydney's man! I was calling to let you know that she doesn't need that fancy car you got her. And to tell you man to man to stay away from my woman."

I could not believe this shit. I did not want any part of the games they were playing. "Look, partna, tell yo' woman to stay away from me. I don't know what games y'all playing over there, but I wants no parts of that shit! You're looking for her, but she ain't here, nigga. Not tonight! How the fuck you get my number anyway?" *Calling me, questioning me about a woman you can't control! Fuck outta here,* I thought.

"It don't matter how I got your number. Just stay away from my woman, and we'll have no need to ever talk again!"

I laughed at this character. I shook my head, listening to his idle threat. "Look, you and my baby momma handle y'all's lil situation without me involved. I don't want her. Now, if you call my house again, you, nigga, are going to have a real problem," I threatened.

I hung up the phone and took a deep breath before I walked out the living room. I didn't like the energy Shorty and her lame were trying to stir up in me. It was drama, and I hated drama. I decided to run upstairs to my bedroom and my stash spot.

"I'll be right back, boo," I yelled to Evelyn.

"C! You're going to miss the whole movie," she yelled back.

"I'm just about to run upstairs and roll up real quick. I need to relax," I yelled at the top of the stairs.

I came back down and entered the den. Evelyn was laid out across my big, brown, leather sofa with a huge bowl of popcorn. I rolled up a stuffed hydro blunt on the coffee table.

"Is everything okay?" Evelyn asked. She sounded just as innocent as the two ponytails looked on her. She had her hair in two long ponytails, one with a white tie and another with a blue tie. The hair accessories accompanied her denim Tommy Hilfiger overalls and matching TH tube top and boxers.

"Yeah, everything good, boo. Nothing to worry about. Just bullshit," I told her as I licked the blunt finished. I sat back on the couch, and she snuggled up under me. I lit my blunt, and within a couple puffs, I forgot about the bullshit with Shorty.

"I can help you relax, C," Evelyn told me as she ran her hands up my chest and down my torso.

As I was inhaling and exhaling the smoke, Evelyn was raising my shirt and tugging at my belt buckle. I assisted her in taking off my belt and undoing my jeans. That was something I was growing to love about her. She was never hesitant with giving me head. And me, I was a sucker for good head. It aroused her intensely, and she wanted to please me.

"I love these briefs on you," she admitted as she began to place kisses along the black Gucci waistband.

She was so soft, and her touch was so gentle. She caressed my erect penis through my boxer briefs as she kissed and licked on my torso. She kissed my chest, licked my neck, and then kissed my lips. She tasted buttery and sweet. She then guided my throbbing penis out of my underwear. She smiled at me before she went to greet him with kisses. She licked her lips and kissed the head, stroking him with burning desire. She opened her mouth and guided my dick in slowly, being sure to lick every inch. Small moans escaped my lips as I could hear her moaning as well. She pulled away, kissed the head, and then deep-throated my whole dick.

"Damn, boo," I whispered, as I could feel her tongue and back throat muscles massaging the tip of my dick.

She licked the shaft all the way back to the head and then looked up to me. I knew she wanted to see my facial expressions. I knew she got a kick out of pleasing me and making me vulnerable in her hands. I looked down to her and grabbed the back of her head. She seductively smiled at me and then put him back in her mouth.

We both got into a rhythm, and I proceeded to fuck her face. She loved that shit. I moaned, and she sucked harder and deeper but never too much harder.

"Um," she moaned as she tongue kissed the tip.

"Suck that dick, boo."

Of course, she obeyed, licking up and down the shaft. She began to stroke him fast and follow it with the same pace of sucking and licking.

"Damn, girl. You gonna make me bust," I admitted, speeding up my pace. I could feel my dick hitting the back of her throat, but it didn't matter. The pure fact of my busting in her mouth motivated her to take as much as she could for as long as she could.

"Shit," I yelled as I snatched her head up.

"What?" she asked, looking up to me.

"Not yet," I replied, shaking my head.

She then stood up and began to undress herself. I reached over to light my blunt. I smoked as I watched her undress. As I inhaled, she slowly slid a condom on me. She then straddled herself over me to welcome me to her wet pussy. I pierced her pussy easily as she slid down slowly.

She rocked her hips, and I pumped as we created a nice, slow motion. She began to speed up as smoke filled the room. Bouncing up and down faster and grinding harder, her ample breasts bounced, and she began to massage and caress them. She licked her nipples and blew kisses at me.

"Oooh shit, C," she screamed as I could feel her body began to climax. Her fingers and toes would wiggle, and she would scream so loud. That would make me fuck her harder.

I flipped her over on the couch to her back as I set the blunt in the ashtray. I put her legs together and bent them back toward her. I was deeper inside her. I could feel her pussy throbbing.

"Yes, C! Yes, C! Ooooh baby," she screamed as I explored.

My pumps grew harder and deeper, and I knew I could no longer hold the nut she was trying to take from me earlier.

"Yes, C! Yes! You in this pussy, baby! Yes," she shouted, squeezing her breasts.

I continued to stroke her slowly and then drill her roughly. The movie finished, credits rolled, and the tape started to rewind itself by the time I busted.

"Aahh," I roared, tightening my grip on her legs.

She immediately jumped off, snatched off the condom, put my dick in her mouth. She was trying to capture all off him. He continued to jump in her mouth as she began to suck out the warm liquid.

I looked down to her with sweat over my brow. "Damn, girl. You trying to make a nigga fall in love?!"

She kissed the head and then smiled at me. "I could say the same to you."

She then crawled back to the top of the couch with me. I held her in my arms as I kissed on her shoulder. The Italian furniture was big enough for us both to lay comfortably.

"It feels good being in your arms," she told me.

"It feels good having you in them. You're so soft," I responded. I ran my hands over her soft skin. I was seeing more and more every day that Evelyn was perfect. She fell asleep quickly, and I was right behind her.

I woke up early enough to start on breakfast for Evelyn. I wasn't a master chef, but if I was hungry, I ate. I loved to read and try new things, so I was always in the kitchen whipping up something. Failure or success was the gamble dish, but it was always worth the try. I heard Evelyn wake up as I stood in the kitchen preparing our meal. I cooked us some scrambled eggs, bacon, and waffles. I also cut up some fresh fruit. Evelyn floated in the kitchen as I was slicing the strawberries.

"Good morning." She spoke softly as she entered.

"Good morning, beautiful. There's some coffee over there if you would like some," I offered as she came over to kiss me.

"Yes, please," she stated as she walked over to the counter. She wore only my sweatshirt and her TH boxers. She poured a glass of black coffee and took a sip.

"No sugar or cream?" I asked.

"No thank you. I like my coffee like I like my man ... strong, black, and hot," she stated as she looked me up and down.

I smiled at her. She walked over to me and hopped up on the oversized island in the middle of the kitchen.

"Last night was ..." she spoke but didn't finish. She just smiled and looked out the window.

"Yes. You were incredible. I'm glad you came over," I replied as I finished cutting the fruit.

"I'm glad you invited me over," she stated with a smile. "I love your kitchen, C! You designed all this? Decorated? Everything," she quizzed, looking around.

"Yeah. The design, layout, and structure ... yes—all me. Of course, I had my crew help, but I hired an interior decorator. I gave her details and ideas, and we came up with this," I replied, looking around. The crisp white paint, dark woods, and marble floors throughout were the perfect neutral background.

"This is a big house for just you. You looking to start a family soon or ..." she inquired, sipping her coffee.

"No. I built this house five years ago. I had my family in here, once. But things didn't work out. I do have other properties elsewhere, but this is my favorite—my first home. I don't know. Maybe one day I'll have a family filling up this big old house. Come on, let's eat. I'm sure you have work, and I got a meeting at nine," I told her as I picked her up off the counter. "Here. Take this and follow me," I instructed as I handed her the glass container filled with orange juice.

I grabbed the tray with the fruit and condiments. I had our table set outside. We walked the gravel path that led to my garden. My courtyard was my quiet sanctuary. It was a beautiful, peaceful morning. I wanted to take full advantage of it with my beautiful woman. We enjoyed our breakfast and made love once more in the shower.

Evelyn walked out the door moments before I did, as I was caught by the telephone.

"Call you later, sugar," Evelyn announced as she slipped through the door.

"C," I answered.

"C, wut up?" I heard Trail say into the phone.

"I was just about to walk out the door. What's going on?"

"Not much. We got a shipment coming in early today. I'll make the run. You close that deal with the rehab job," he negotiated.

"Okay, cool. We'll rap later," I told him and then hung up.

I walked out the door and hopped in my black on black BMW 740Li. I arrived at my office building in record time. Luckily, I arrived before nine o'clock. Traffic wasn't as heavy as I thought it would be.

"Good morning, Mr. Stone. I have a few messages for you. Your two o'clock tomorrow wants to get pushed up to eleven that morning, and you have a dentist appointment approaching," my secretary, Ebony, informed me as I got settled into my office.

I set my briefcase on my desk. She continued to read off more messages as I took a seat in my merlot-colored leather chair.

"Sunshine today, Mr. Stone?" she asked as she walked over to the windows.

"Yes, it's going to be a beautiful day," I answered her.

She proceeded to open the blinds on the floor-to-ceiling windows. "Do you need anything, Mr. Stone? Coffee or breakfast?" she asked.

"No thank you, Ebony. I'm good. Let me get ready for the meeting. Inform me when my nine o'clock gets here. No calls until my meeting is over," I directed.

"Yes, will do," she replied and exited.

I had my presentation prepared based on the budget my client submitted. This was going to be a huge job for my company and could have me out of town for months on end, but I was ready to tackle this big project and take this huge payout. I had recently become state certified and obtained my Unlimited License, and I was ready to utilize it. My clients were right on time.

"Carleon! Good to see you, buddy," Marc greeted. He was an old college associate. He was also the owner of the complex we were about to rehabilitate.

"Marc, what's going on?"

We slapped fives and shook hands. He was just as excited as I was, and we got right to business. They were pleased with the numbers. I could understand and deliver his ideas.

"Yep, I knew to come here. Not only are you listening to give me exactly what I want, but you've found ways to save money and still be within code. I knew I had to come to you to get the job done right," he told me.

"I appreciate that. I'm just here to do a quality job and make my clients happy."

The meeting ended great. We planned to break ground in a month and celebrate later tonight. The meeting ended around lunchtime, but I decided to stay in for lunch. Ebony went to get me a sandwich from the sub shop down the street. I worked on the schedules, contracts, and spec sheets to plan for the new job. I was always a compulsive worker. Once I got started on something, it was almost impossible for me to stop. There were many nights I was the last person in the office. I would complete an entire week's work in one day.

"Mr. Stone, are you going to enjoy the sunset, or would you like for me to close the blinds," Ebony asked, standing in the doorway.

I didn't even realize the day had passed. I finished the entire expense report, finalized budgets, and had most local contractors lined up for work.

"No, I'll get them, Ebony. Enjoy your evening," I declared, swamped in paperwork.

"Okay, Mr. Stone. Good night," she parted.

I stood up to walk to my bar. I poured myself a small glass of cognac, went to my stereo, and put in some classical music. I enjoyed all the classic, great composers. I relished in nocturnes from Chopin or sonatas from Beethoven. Classical music relaxed me. I loved how the music started slow and soft. Then it could become so intense and dramatic. It could come off as emotionless or full of emotion. I appreciated the heartfelt strums of a string quartet or the bold chords from a piano. A beautiful composition could demonstrate a broken heart or an enormous success. Starting with just a simple melody and ending in a daring symphony, it made me enjoy the moment in tranquility.

I looked out the window and adored the sunset. It was a beautiful view of the city. The landscape was lovely from my corner office. I loosened my tie and took a sip of the warm brandy. My private line then rang. It was after hours, but apparently, someone knew I was here.

I walked over to answer the phone. "Hello?"

"C, wut up? How'd the meeting go?" Trail inquired over the other end.

"You know I executed that. What's up with the delivery?" I quizzed as I took a seat at my desk.

"Right on time. I'm thinking we'll have everything broke down and distributed by the weekend. When you leaving the office?"

"I'm about to finish up and meet Marc at the bar. Swing through. Marc love dat white girl. Bring some party favors," I suggested.

"I got you," Trail stated.

Our conversation was then ended. I looked at the phone and wanted to call my baby. I wanted to hear her voice. However, I didn't want to rap with Shorty. After that bullshit last night, I was done with her games. I picked up the phone and called my daughter. The phone rang a few times while I sipped my drink.

"Hello," Shorty spoke into the phone.

"Shorty, what up?" I replied.

"Wow. Hey, C."

"What's the *wow* for?" I chuckled.

"Oh, nothing. Just surprised you calling."

"Yeah. I mean, no need for us to have animosity. We good, right?"

"Yeah, we good. I should apologize for interrupting you last night. I didn't mean any harm by it. I really did just want to thank you for the car," she told me.

I knew her form of thanking me was coming over to my house and showing me just how thankful she really was. "It's all good, Shorty. What we had was great. We got a beautiful daughter, and we still have our great friendship. Things are changing. We are changing," I told her.

I knew I was changing. I could see it day by day. I was ready to love again. I was ready to be faithful again. It was time to focus on all the positives and the future. I couldn't waste any more time or energy dwelling on past regrets.

"Yeah, you're right about that. I decided to keep the baby. I told Ryan last night," she informed me. I could hear the relief in her tone.

"Oh. So, how did that go?" I asked, curious. I took a sip of my cognac as I listened to her talk.

"It went well. He's extremely happy. But he feels that because I'm pregnant, we're automatically supposed to be together," she replied.

"Shit, I thought y'all were together," I declared.

"No, we're not official. We never were. We were just kicking it. I fucked up and got pregnant," she admitted.

"Damn. Well, I do wish you the best of luck. Regardless of the situation, you know I will always be there for you," I let her know. I meant that. I didn't care if she was expecting with another man or married, we would always have our bond. I would always be there for Shorty.

"Thank you, C. I appreciate you so much. You are truly a blessing. I hope whatever woman gets you, loves and appreciates you. You deserve it and so much more," she said.

"I appreciate that, Shorty," I told her.

Her words really felt sincere and genuine. After three years of our separation, I finally got the apology I felt I needed to move on. Lessons were everywhere in life, even in the failed relationship Shorty and I now shared. Mistakes must be embraced to grow.

"I was calling to talk to Cupcake. And to tell you I just took on a huge project. I leave in the next month or so. I'll be out of town for a few months," I stated.

"Dang … months?! Well, congratulations. I'm sure Cupcake is going to miss you. She's next door at a playdate. I'll have her call you once she makes it home. Oh, and thanks again for the car," she told me.

"Happy birthday again. Have her call me tomorrow. Good night, Shorty."

Our conversation was then ended. I closed my blinds and began to shut down my office. I grabbed my suit coat and briefcase as I headed out the door. I got into my sleek vehicle and headed to the bar. I planned on enjoying the evening and all the success in my life. Life was good, and I was grateful. I walked into the bar on a positive vibe and planned to walk out on an even higher one.

CHAPTER 15

Four Months Later

January 6, 1999. It had been one of the coldest winters ever. It was my sweet Cupcake's birthday. I was near end of my third trimester, almost nine months pregnant and ready to pop. I dropped my baby off at school and headed home to relax for a few hours. There was a bone-chilling wind and the streets were covered in faint snow. Cupcake requested dinner with her mother and father for her seventh birthday. C had been out of town for the past few months, and she was anticipating enjoying being the only child. I knew she wanted this quality time with both her parents before the baby came.

I pulled into my driveway after the short drive from Cupcake's school. I walked into the house and flopped onto the couch. My ankles were getting so swollen. My telephone then rang.

"Hello," I answered.

"Good morning, beautiful! How are you and my baby?" Ryan asked from the other end.

I couldn't believe he was calling as if everything were fine. Weeks after I told Ryan about the pregnancy, he became extremely possessive and obsessive. When I told him I was pregnant, he was ecstatic! I didn't want to ruin the occasion for him, so I never told him my doubts about his paternity. It's a good thing I didn't because I feel that would've made things much worse. Ryan started stalking me, hiding in my bushes, and playing on C's phone. It was ridiculous.

A small part of me wanted the baby to be C's. I guess I wanted that last spark of hope that we could get back together. But my heart told me this baby belonged to Ryan. In the beginning, I could see a life with Ryan. But as time progressed, he showed traits of possession and anger that I was not used to. I tried to express to him that just because I was pregnant did not mean we were meant to be together.

He would always reply with, "Sydney, you're just not ready yet. I'm willing to wait for you because we're meant to be together forever."

"We're great, Ryan. You know you are not supposed to be in contact with me," I answered.

"Anyway ... I know today is Cupcake's birthday, so I was thinking we can take her shopping and to One Stop tonight," he told me proudly.

I wasn't ready for whatever family playdate he'd obviously made up in his head. "That sounds fun, but you know we can't do that. We're having dinner with C tonight," I informed him.

"What?! What do you mean we're? He's not even here! Why would you need to go anyway?" he demanded.

This is how Ryan reacted anytime C's name was mentioned or brought up. I couldn't take his imaginary individual competition he had with C.

"Ryan, he's back in town for Cupcake's birthday. Why am I even explaining this to you?! C is Cori's father. He will *always* be around. He will always be in my life."

Ryan was silent, and so was I.

"Ryan, it's too early for all this. You trying to start something over nothing. This is not worth an argument because it will never change. The restraining order still stands. I will contact you once the baby is born," I suggested.

"Whatever, Sydney," he stated and then hung up the phone.

I could sense that he was upset about the dinner date with my family later. Frankly, I didn't care. I wasn't going to entertain Ryan's behavior. It had been weeks since I'd filed the order and seen him.

I decided to cook myself breakfast as I stood up from the couch. This pregnancy had my appetite all crazy. I wanted pancakes, fried pork chops, mashed potatoes, and cheesy scrambled eggs. I went into my kitchen and whipped up that exact menu. When I was done, I opened my blinds and took a seat at my breakfast table. I looked out the window as I stuffed my mouth with pork chops and eggs. The snow was so pretty—white and crisp. It seemed so peaceful with light sunrays hitting the blankets of snow.

I seasoned this pork chop so good, I thought as I ate a forkful with some pancake. I was interrupted from devouring my breakfast when the phone rang. I decided to let the answering machine get it. After I heard the beep, I listened for the message.

"Shorty, what's up, love? Just calling to let you know my flight touches down 'round one o'clock. I'll get Cupcake from school, and then we'll come scoop you and head on out," C spoke.

I smiled just hearing him say my name. C would always have that effect on me—his voice, his presence, his touch. I would always regret taking a good man like C for granted. I ruined a beautiful relationship with a king and ended up with a toxic connection to a joker. That's karma for you.

I finished up my breakfast and wished I would've cooked two chops as I sucked on the bone. I cleaned up the kitchen and wiped down the table and then headed to my bedroom to rest. I turned on the TV and laid across my bed. The heat had my home nice and cozy. I grabbed my fuzzy fleece throw from the end of my bed to cover my body. I was going to sneak in a quick nap before Cupcake's outing tonight. She had a big circus-themed birthday bash planned at her favorite park for the weekend. I wanted her to enjoy a day of fun with all her friends and cousins. The afternoon talk show played in the background as I began to doze off.

A vivid nightmare woke me from my sleep. My pregnancy brought along a lot of strange, weird dreams, but that one was eerie. I couldn't remember it entirely, but I did remember watching my baby cry as she was being taken from me. I shook off the discomfort from the dream as I sat up in bed.

My hair was all over my head. I hadn't cut it at all during my pregnancy, and it was now below my shoulders. I looked over and could see my reflection in the mirror from my dresser. My face was fat, and my lips were bigger. Luckily, my nose didn't spread. But it didn't matter. I was a beautiful pregnant woman. I could see my glow shining back at me in the mirror. I smiled.

During the past year, I'd learn to embrace my scars. I learned to not hide behind my scars. Those four grazes didn't make me, and my decisions from that dreadful night didn't define me. I had been too hard on myself for a very long time, and I had to let go of that. I was learning to put the consequences of that night into perspective. I wasn't a victim or a villain. I just learned to forgive myself and accept my path. I set free the hurt, shame and guilt of that night.

It was hard, but I had to also accept the fact that C may never forgive me. But it was okay. He didn't have to. The most important thing was that I had finally forgiven myself, and I knew regardless that he still loved me. C was a good man to me and would always be a good man. I knew he would always be there for me. And for that, I was grateful.

I got up and proceeded to the bathroom to take a nice hot bubble bath. I slipped into the tub and enjoyed the hot water. It felt so good against my skin. I looked down at my huge stomach and rubbed it. I could then feel my son moving around. It was as if he moved to my touch every time. He would move whenever I sang to him. We had a bond, a connection already. I sat and watched him do tricks in my belly as the water cooled.

My doorbell rang, and momentarily, I could hear my baby girl yelling, "Mommy!"

I hurried up, washed up, and exited the bathroom. I put on a pair of comfy maternity jeans and a white Chanel cashmere sweater. I brushed my hair in a ponytail and braided it. I felt beautiful, so I decided not to put on any makeup. I put on a pair of white snow boots and exited my bedroom.

C and Cupcake were playing in the living room. Her laughter filled the room along with several "Happy Birthday" balloons.

"Sounds like the birthday girl is here," I sang, walking down the hallway to the living room.

C had her held in the air like a superhero as he lay on his back.

"Mommy, Mommy," Cupcake screamed once she saw me. She hurriedly jumped out of C's arms and ran to me. She was getting taller as the days were getting longer. She was almost at my waistline. I knew she was going to be taller than me, and from the looks of it, it would be pretty soon.

C sat up and spoke. "Shorty, what's up, girl?"

"Hey, C. Welcome back!"

"Mommy, Daddy came back for my birthday! I told you he was coming, Mommy," she gushed as she ran to her father. She jumped on his back and pretended she was riding a horse. I laughed as they continued to play on the floor.

"Okay, okay, baby. Let's go get something to eat and get you some birthday cake," C told her as he stood up.

"Yay! Okay, Daddy! Let's go, Momma," Cupcake announced.

"Okay, do you need to go to the bathroom first?" I asked her.

"Oh, yep! Be right back," she stated as she ran down the hallway.

C turned to me and looked down to my huge belly. "Whoa, Shorty. I know I've been gone for a few months, but I swear it look like you blew up overnight," he declared, reaching to rub my belly.

His huge hand covered the top of my stomach. I felt him kick. "Lil man kicking my hand off, huh?" C joked, pulling away.

I laughed, and he flashed his beaming, beautiful smile. "Well, you've been gone for four months. I never saw you when you came those few weekends. And when you sent for Cupcake, you literally sent for her. I didn't see you," I informed him with a small laugh.

C had been in and out of town for four consecutive months, rehabbing an apartment complex. He would send for Cupcake to spend some weekends with him up there. He made quick home appearances, but he left just as quickly. I felt like maybe he was avoiding me and my pregnancy. However, I later learned he was involved with that beautiful woman from the club. I wasn't jealous or resentful. Upon investigation of the chick, I was actually happy for C. She appeared to be a successful, good woman.

"Yeah, I'm almost done up there. Well, for the most part. I just needed to be present for the initial stage of the rehab. I'll be home for good in a few weeks."

"Mommy! Daddy! I'm ready," Cupcake shouted. She ran to the couch to put on her coat and hat.

"Come here, baby. Let me help you with your gloves," C told her. He knelt to assist her with her little mittens.

I got my purse and coat off the coat hanger near the front door. I reached to open the door, and Ryan rushed in through the doorway. He pushed past me, almost causing me to fall to the floor.

"Ryan, what the hell?!" I yelled.

"Well aren't y'all just the happy fucking family here," he slurred.

I could smell the scent of alcohol the more he spoke.

"Aw … Mommy, Daddy, Cupcake, and baby. The perfect family, huh? I guess me coming along messed up everything, huh, C? Sydney?" he asked, looking toward me.

Cupcake was standing behind her father, and C looked confused.

"Ryan, what are you doing here?! You know you're not supposed to be here! What is wrong with you?" I demanded.

He looked at me and smiled. The handsome gentleman I once saw was not the person looking back at me. Ryan looked angry and possessed. I could see that he was drunk as well.

"What am I doing here?! What am I doing here?! No, Sydney! What the fuck is *he* doing here?! Every time it's anything involving him, you're fucking lying," he screamed.

I had never seen him this outraged. I didn't understand his behavior.

"Look, partna, we about to go. So, you can just—" C began to state, but once Ryan revealed his .38 revolver, he was silenced.

For a split second, I felt my heart completely stop. Once I saw the shiny piece of metal jammed in his pants, my breathing slowed.

"Oh, so you're quiet now. Yeah! Just shut the fuck up, C," Ryan yelled.

My baby began to cover her face, and small cries escaped her mouth.

"Ryan, can you please calm down? Why are you doing this?" I cried. I could feel tears fill my eyes, but I didn't feel them hit my cheeks.

"Why am I doing this?! No! Why the fuck are you always lying? You tell me you're going to dinner, but you're here having a family-of-the-year moment. So, what's the story today, Sydney?! You ready to tell me you were fucking him while you were fucking me?! You ready to tell me you're still in love with him?! You ready to admit this might not even be my baby?" he roared, pointing the gun at me.

I looked at him and couldn't even see his face anymore. I was at a loss for words. Once upon a time, I could look in his face and smile.

Today, I didn't see his face. I didn't see anything—just the barrel of the gun starting back at me.

"Ryan, please … Put the gun down. You're scaring my baby. Let's talk about this," I pleaded with him.

"Don't cry, Sydney. Everything is going to be okay. I love you. I would never hurt you or your baby," he told me. He sounded so sincere. I believed him for a second, yet he was so erratic.

"Ryan, this is not love. This is possessive. This is toxic … Ryan, this is deadly," I declared.

"Toxic?" he huffed. He scratched his head with the loaded gun. "No, Sydney. My love for you is unconditional, protective, genuine! You been playing with my feelings long enough, Sydney."

I looked over to C, and I could see the frustration in his face. I could sense that he wanted to take on Ryan, but he was too unpredictable.

"C, I will blow yo' mutha fucking head off if you take one step," he threatened as he pointed the gun to him.

"Ryan, please stop this. We are not together! You have no reason to do all this," I interjected.

"See, there you go with all that bullshit again, Sydney. We're basically in a fucking relationship. I don't know why you tiptoe around the fact or pick and choose when it's convenient for you, but we're basically together," he yelled.

"Basically, and officially are two totally different things—literally, Ryan! You need to leave right now, or I'm calling the police," I spoke.

There was a gunshot. It all happened so fast that I didn't see what happened or if anyone was shot, but I did feel something. I dropped everything. My purse and my coat fell to the ground. It felt like someone threw a brick at my chest, and the sharp part hit me hard. It knocked the breath out of me for a second. Everything seemed as if it were happening in slow motion.

The piercing sound of my daughter screaming broke my daze. I looked over to my daughter, and tears flooded from her face. Ryan's voice was going in and out by the time I noticed the blood on my sweater. I fell to the floor and touched my chest. I saw my daughter attempt to run to me, and then I saw Ryan raise the gun to her.

"No! Be still, Cupcake. Mommy's okay. We're about to leave, so you guys have to stay here," I heard him tell my daughter.

I could hear C and Ryan yelling, but I couldn't make out the words. I could barely keep my eyes open as the warm blood drenched my sweater. I heard another gunshot and more yelling. I then blacked out.

When I opened my eyes, Ryan was standing over me. "Sydney! We'll always be together. Forever. I love you," Ryan spoke.

Then there was another gunshot. I saw Ryan's lifeless body fall to the floor.

I blacked out.

"Stay with me, Shorty. Stay with me," I heard C repeating.

I looked up to see him hovered over me, applying pressure to my chest. I blacked out.

"Shorty! Shorty, open your eyes," C yelled.

The loud bass from the music woke me up. I opened my eyes and saw that I was in the back of C's SUV. He was up front driving, and I was laid across the back seat.

"Stay with me, Shorty," he ordered. He turned down the volume of the radio.

"No, no, C. Turn the music back up," I told him softly. "Remember, this used to be our song," I replied. I could feel blood filling my mouth.

"Shorty, please just stay up. Don't go to sleep. Don't close your eyes," he pleaded.

"I won't, C. Remember this song? We were so in love, C," I declared, listening to Jodeci's "Forever My Lady."

You and I
Would never fall apart, baby
You and I
Said we knew right from the start
The day
We fell so far in love
Now our baby is born
Healthy and strong....

CHAPTER 16

Pow! The room was spinning. He turned and pulled the trigger on Shorty. The bullet hit her hard, and she took a few steps back. The tiny hole in middle of her white sweater became red and continued to grow. My daughter began to scream uncontrollably, trying to run to her mother. Ryan then turned the gun to her.

"What the fuck?" I yelled. He had his pistol pointed at my baby girl.

"What?! What the fuck you gonna do now, C?!" he stated.

He began to mumble some crazy shit to Cupcake, as I watched Shorty fall to the ground. She looked so helpless. I felt horrible that I couldn't do anything. I just watched this man shoot the woman he claims to love, while she's pregnant with his baby. He pulled the gun on my child, and I was fearful that he would pull the trigger on her as well. No doubt about it. I felt defenseless as I stood there at gunpoint with my daughter.

"She's dying, man! You need to call the ambulance," I yelled to him.

He looked over to Shorty and smiled. "She's okay. You don't have to worry about her anymore," he replied in a calming tone.

In a flash, he looked away, and in that instant, I rushed him. We tussled for a few seconds, as I attempted to attack him. Cupcake continued to cry louder. I tried to grab the gun, and he pulled the trigger.

"Damn," I shouted. The bullet grazed the side of my left hand. Blood was now dripping from my hand.

My daughter screamed, as I looked over to Shorty. She was trying to keep her eyes open, fighting for her life.

136

"C, don't move nigga! I will shoot your fucking daughter! Just stay out of this … That's what you should've done from the beginning. But no … You have to be *the man* no man can live up to. Well fuck you, C," he yelled.

He then started to pace the floor. "So, you and Cupcake just stay right here! I'll check on Sydney," he ordered.

"Daddy," she cried.

I pulled her into my arms. My hand was bloody, but she needed to feel my protection. I held her tight, as I didn't want her to see her mother like that.

Ryan stood over Shorty, watching her fight as he quietly spoke to her. Then there was a gunshot. His body fell onto the floor, landing next to Shorty. The blood poured from his open skull.

Cupcake began to scream louder. Everything was moving so quickly. The entire moment appeared in fast-forward. As I was running Cupcake out of the house, neighbors were approaching. I handed Cupcake to Shorty's next-door neighbor and then ran back into the house to help Shorty. She was laid out in her own pool of blood. Her once-white sweater was blood red. Her eyes were closed.

I spoke, and she opened her eyes. I knew waiting for the ambulance would be a gamble. I scooped her in my arms and put her in the back seat of my Denali.

"Call the police," I yelled to the onlookers as I drove off.

★★★★★

Shit. He looked just like Shorty. His brown eyes and brown curly hair were the signature look from his mother. He looked more like her than our daughter. They both shared her dominant features and now a birthday.

I held her son, as I watched her body lie on the hospital bed. I felt like I lost a small piece of my heart, as I watched her last breath leave her body. The doctors were unable to save Shorty, but fortunately, the baby was perfectly fine. I still had her blood on my clothes, as I soothed her son.

I was at a loss for words. I couldn't believe what I had just witnessed. I couldn't believe my daughter had to witness this. I shook my head, and I could feel my emotions boiling inside me. I was angry. I was sad. I was hurt.

I couldn't believe that boy took my Shorty away from me. I couldn't believe he would do such a thing in front of our child. Hell, she was pregnant with their baby! I just couldn't digest any of it. A part of me felt guilty. I knew he wasn't right. I knew he didn't deserve Shorty. But my pride wouldn't let me tell her any of that. I didn't want to be against the first guy she fell for after us. But now, I know I should've said something, sooner.

If I would've just said something, anything ... This could've been different, I thought.

Shorty didn't deserve this. Shorty was so special. She meant so much to me. I held back my tears and wished I could've said more, wished I could've done more.

"Sir, we need to take the baby for some tests," the nurse came to tell me.

I could barely control my movement. I couldn't even control my emotions. Tears began to fall as she took the baby from my arms.

"Sir, are you the father?" she asked.

ABOUT THE BOOK

Pride is an emotion, as well as a devotion. To stand by your pride could leave you standing all alone …

How easy is it to apologize for hurting someone you love? How simple would it be to accept that apology?

This is the tale of two lovers told from both sides. Shorty deals with guilt, while C is haunted by his pride. She may see it one way, which could appear different in his eyes. Yet, in reality, there's always truth and lies.

Follow me to the '90.

Printed in the United States
By Bookmasters